The Mothers

Nollaig Frost

Published by New Generation Publishing in 2021

First Edition

ISBN
     Paperback   978-1-80031-463-4
     Hardback   978-1-80031-462-7
     Ebook   978-1-80031-461-0

Front cover photograph:
'Fairy Pond in County Cork' ©Anne-Marie O'Mahony

www.newgeneration-publishing.com

 New Generation Publishing

For Eleanor
With thanks for my London life and my Irish roots, and
the family and friends that both have brought

"I don't believe in fairies but I know that they're there"

Chapter 1

The cobalt chill of a rare cloudless sky prickles my skin as I step out of the lake. The squelch of mud between my toes is oddly comforting and I stop to throw my head back and inhale the peat-scented air. Its salty tang brushes my lips and I feel it infusing my body with energy. I know I am going to need this energy when I reach the house again, and I take an extra breath. My insides warm as my skin chills and I tell myself to put one foot in front of the other to walk back up through the meadow.

He is at the front door when I arrive, and I can see that he is in a sulk. His father's eyes glare at me from beneath a pudding bowl of rust-coloured hair. His round face has a hint of crimson at the cheeks, contrasting with the milky whiteness of skin that I know would be soft if he allowed me to touch it.

'Where's my breakfast?' he says, 'I couldn't find you. Where have you been?'

'You know where I've been, Max, where I always am before breakfast, swimming in the lake. You should come with me one morning,'

I know that he won't but dread that one day he will confound me, not for the first time in his seven years, by agreeing, just to spite me.

'Well I'm hungry,' he says, stomping off, too-small tartan pyjamas flapping around short pale legs. I watch him disappear into the vastness of the house, trying to feel again the caress of the water, wishing for the peace that it brings me. I fail, and grabbing my dressing gown from the hallway hook, I follow him to the Aga warmth of the basement kitchen.

#

Later, sitting in my dressing gown at the kitchen table with the lingering smell of scrambled eggs and baked beans only just masked by coffee fumes, I treat myself to the fantasy that Conor is still here. I picture the mop of his copper-coloured hair, much more vivid that Max's pale imitation, unbrushed and ruffled as he would appear at the kitchen door, lured by the breakfast odours, strong enough to waft up three floors to our bedroom. I see him flicking it back with a toss of his head as he leans in to kiss me, and the half-smile that promises understanding and support in the challenge of parenting Max. Lifting my cup for a sip I see his photo, still prominent in the jumble of second-hand teacups, bills, and empty vases on the dresser. There is the hair, the half-smile, the reassurance, but still, unmoving and silent. This morning it is not comforting. Nor does it anger me. This morning I am worn down and send yet another signal to say that he can come home now. That wherever he has been, whatever he has been doing, we can work it out. Conor can come home to me and meet the child he has never known.

Here is Max back, hair brushed, school uniform on, bag in hand.

'It's time for school, come on, let's go,' he says with that haughtiness that makes me feel like his servant rather than his mother.

'Max, I'm not even dressed yet, we have plenty of time. You stay and read your book; I'll be back down in a minute.'

Pushing myself up from the table, cup in hand I shuffle in slippered feet towards the door, me with head down, he, upright in the large high-backed wooden chair, legs dangling, book perched on school bag on lap, looking like he is seated on a throne.

My heavy tread up the six steps leading to the magnificent hall is harmonised by the creak of the floorboards. Each groan and squeak loses itself in the empty space, reminding me that we are only two in this place, big enough for fifty, longing for three. Once a grand hotel, the house begs for more life than Max and I can offer it. It yearns for new life, for noise, for people, but it is drained of energy and its listlessness matches mine.

At the start Conor and I nurtured the house. We dreamed of its recovery, enthused about breathing new energy into it, of filling it with our lives. True, we spent more hours imagining every detail than actually working on making them real, but our vigour seeped into the walls, infiltrated the elegant arches, plumped it up. Only that was seven years ago. Now, Max and I, and the house, struggle to maintain any life at all. We teeter on the edge of the Conor-shaped hole at its centre, resenting each other for his absence. Unused rooms sink into their tattered wallpaper and fraying curtains and resign themselves to redundancy. The ones we live in are scant in furniture and crowded with memories. High ceilings, and uneven floors mock us as we huddle, separate from each other, in the same confined space.

Infusing the house with a life of its own is a habit I picked up from Conor. He gave each room a name, mimicking the trend for naming offices rather than numbering them. He called them after his psychology heroes: the kitchen, the room he saw as becoming the centre of the house, was Freud, obviously; the drawing room was the softer Winnicott; the cold utility room, Klein; and the bedroom where our baby would be made, Bowlby. The dining room was Pavlov. Conor said that one day we would get a dog, an Irish wolfhound, to reflect both the grandeur of the house, and our heritage, and use the empty dining room to train it in so we could call it Pavlov's dog. The five acres of grounds he refused to name, instead always referring to them as 'the Context', explaining that to label its woods, meadows, lawns and lake would be to suggest that each was separate when in fact all depended on each other in order to thrive. 'A bit like the two of us,' he used to say. The funny thing is that, by naming the rooms, Conor has left me with yet another reason to feel guilty Instead of feeding these eminent psychologists with rich and varied emotions I am allowing them to die around me.

Dressed now in the green pinafore that is so easy to throw over whatever I happen to put on each day and still look respectable, I slip double-socked feet into wellington boots, comfy and good preparation for the mud outside. As I tramp down the stairs calling Max I hear nothing, but there he is in the hallway waiting by the front door, annoyed that he is still too short to reach up and open it.

Making our way across the potholed courtyard to the car, I try conversation, 'So what are you going to do at school today?'

Silence. I give it another go, 'Who are you going to play with?'

He knows this is a silly question. I know it too, but I ask it most days, hoping that eventually he will say something to reassure me. I know Max has no friends, and I know why. Max is the child whose father disappeared when his mother was pregnant. The child who is being brought up in a single-parent household because, so they say, his mother drove his father away. The child who is different, cold, and hostile, and not a little frightening. Nobody wants to be his friend.

At the end of the driveway I drag open the ornate black iron gates that secure the entrance, leaving the car running. We drive through in silence, the ancient Volvo wheezing and belching until it reaches the tarmac road which sneers at the unmade track we have just so carefully navigated. One day the car too will die, I just hope it does it with some consideration for me and not at a time when I am in the middle of town.

I dread the trips to town, the whispers and the stares. I know what people think about me. When Conor first disappeared I expected sympathy. I would have welcomed it; I felt sorry for myself, alone and pregnant. Now I prefer to be alone. I have learnt that stories of tragedy invite judgement rather than understanding. It was decided then that I did something to drive Conor away and his disappearance became my fault for turning a good man into a feckless one.

The small market town with narrow rows of houses on narrow streets, has only one school. It is where all the children of the town and its surrounding areas are educated, and from where the information about all that happens in those areas emanates. The information spreads into the shops, the pubs, the gym where the mothers dash after dropping off their children, and to the coffee shops where they sip their reward after their exertions. The information becomes fact, is embellished and shared. To be discussed there is to be both recognised and vilified. Max and I had been discussed there since he started at the nursery five years ago.

We draw up in the car and without a word to me, his taxi driver, Max leaps out and marches in through the gates. As I start to pull away, relieved at not catching the eye of any of the gaggle standing around the school entrance, the head teacher's red, round face appears in my rear-view mirror. He is calling and waving at me with an urgency that can mean only one thing. With a sigh I pull in again and step out, decorating my face with a smile that hovers only around my mouth.

'Mr Murphy, good morning.'

'Yes, er good morning Mrs Fairman, um, can I have a quick word?'

I feel the familiar lurch in my stomach and tense my muscles to stand and listen to the usual words: 'challenging', 'aggressive', upsetting other children', 'it can't go on'. I rearrange my face into my earnest-mother look. I agree, I nod, I look serious. All the while a clenching in my chest begs him not to suspend Max. I cannot, simply cannot, have my seven hours a day without him compromised.

Eventually Mr Murphy concludes.

'So we must keep a close eye on Max. I will meet with him weekly and remind him of the importance of playing nicely with the other children.'

My muscles relax and I fawn my thanks, trying not to give away my relief. I smile again, this time more sincerely, and hasten back to the car. Once safely out of earshot, on the final stretch of country road that takes me back to the house, I turn up the radio and sing along out loud to 'Club Tropicana'.

The gates to the house are open, I must have forgotten to close them. Ever since that night when I saw lights in the woods, I have heaved them shut after me when I leave or enter. I still hear sounds, sometimes coming from the grounds, sometimes from inside the house, but I tell myself I must be imagining them, and dismiss them without fear. Inside those gates I know that the water of the lake loves me, the Ash trees and Olearias don't judge me, the stone walls protect me. I can roam and think and reminisce, wandering in 'the Context' and dreaming of what might have been. On good days I convince myself that Conor will return, that there will be an explanation for him leaving, and that we can resume the life we had, even with Max in it. It is odd that I did not close them today, but I suppose the distraction of attempting conversation with Max means I forgot.

There is a strange scent in the air as I drive up the track. I don't recognise it. It is sulphurous, unpleasant. I roll up the car window and it fogs over, so I am slow to see the figure standing in front of the house. A man, his back to me, is standing and shuffling from foot to foot, staring up at the house. I notice that he is wearing only one trainer, the other foot bare. He is tall and gaunt with lank, unkempt, long greying hair straggling over a tattered mud-spattered raincoat. I hear a keening sound.

'Hello, can I help you? This is private property you know.'

No response, only the musical murmuring. I call again, louder, but stay close to the car for some sort of faux protection.

'Er hello, are you lost? Are you looking for someone? Can I help?'

My voice bounces back, mingling with the indecipherable words coming from him. Are they Gaelic? Unusual but not unheard of round here. I can't quite make them out but they prod some distant memory of Irish language lessons at school.

With the man's lack of response, I feel braver, and loosen my hold on the car's roof to approach him. The crunch of my feet on the gravel is invasive, even to me, cutting across the singing, challenging action. It is only when I am two footsteps behind him that the man turns around. I see his eyes first, those emerald eyes, the colour of my engagement ring bought to match them. His face is grey, masked with a dull sheen of exhaustion. His hands are bunched at the end of straight arms hanging by his side. I see small rips and tears peppering the raincoat, and notice that his jeans too are torn. When he looks at me the keening stops. As I meet his eyes we are shrouded by a stillness. Nothing else exists, only me and him. We are in a hold, tighter than any I have felt for seven years. My body is rigid. I feel a storm coming in the too-still air but I can't move. He and I are transfixed until the ugly squawk of a crow circling above us bursts through the silence.

'I'm sorry,' he says.

As raindrops begin to ping off the leaves of the trees high above us I begin to melt. Heat surges through me and relief creeps around the edges of my hardness. He staggers the two steps towards me and starts to fall. I step forward to catch him and without any more thought lead my husband into our house.

#

The storm when it comes is like the one on the night that Conor disappeared. As usual we had spent the day planning a lot and doing very little on the house. As usual he had asked if I wanted to go to the pub with him, because he thought it important to get to know people. As usual, I was happy for him to go without me. I said I wanted to catch up on some of my neglected, guilt-inducing PhD work. We kissed each other and as usual, I warned him to be careful coming back in the dark, to remember to take a torch. Conor laughed and I laughed too as I watched him ease the huge front door open with one swing of his muscular arm and bounce out of it.

I waited five minutes, pacing the room, closing half-open drawers, putting the tops back onto toiletries. When I was sure he had gone, I crossed the landing to the bathroom, locked the door and opened the pregnancy kit I had bought yesterday.

When it showed positive, excitement danced its way from my stomach up through my chest and onto my face. It consumed my body. Bodies. It had happened. Finally, we were pregnant. The last piece of the dream had fallen into place.

It was so hard to wait for Conor to get back. To wait to watch him as I told him the news. To wait to feel him lift me up, whirl me round, kiss me. He would probably want to make love and with a little hesitation we would fall into bed in Bowlby.

To urge the time to pass I turned up the music on the small portable speaker that moved around the house with us and made a surprise dinner. I dug out Great Aunt Alice's Irish linen tablecloth and spread it on Pavlov's bare floorboards. I dressed it with candles and plates of cheese and salmon and bread. The beating of the wind on the inadequate single-glazed windows did not bother me, nor did the driving rain that I knew would find the leak in the bathroom ceiling before the night was out. Nothing bothered me. I was pregnant. Wonderfully, joyfully pregnant.

It was when the candles started guttering, wisps of smoke curling in the half darkness of the room, their dying smell mixing with that of warm smoked salmon and softening cheese to send signals of nausea to my stomach, that those wild elements did start bothering me. For the first time in the house I began to feel fear. It wrapped itself around my two bodies with tendrils that gripped and squeezed more and more tightly as the time passed. My head felt heavy and the sound of blood coursing through it amplified the whistles and bangs of the wind and the battering of the rain at the windows seeking entry. Something was wrong. Conor should be back by now.

I remember the panicked run I made down the driveway, even then holding my stomach to protect the pea-sized life inside it, cursing the lost buttons on my coat. I remember my breath coming heavy as I thought I would never reach the end of the endless dark ribbon of road. I remember pushing open the heavy door of the pub, stumbling in and seeing the blank faces of the men that peered at me from under wisps of hair hovering over half-finished pints. I remember their silence and the meaningless reassurance of the barmaid that he was most likely home by now, left ages ago, probably took the shortcut across the fields. I know I wanted to believe her but knew inside that she was wrong. I remember longing for Conor to appear from the bathroom and look at me with surprise as he zipped up his jeans.

But he didn't, and he wasn't, and now, seven years after that night, he is collapsed in our bed, exhausted and without explanation. He has said nothing except 'sorry' since we came into the house, and even that was whispered and forced. As I stand over his sleeping form I want to shake him awake, to demand to know, beg to be told, where he has been. I want to hold him, to hit him, to shout at him but I can do nothing. My husband has returned, and I am still alone.

Chapter 2

I tiptoe into the bedroom, as I have done the past two mornings since Conor's return. Its thin curtains are drawn against the creeping light of late morning and I take a sharp breath as the sour odour of dirt and sweat sweeps into my nostrils. I move with caution towards the bed and the hump under the heap of duvet that I can just make out. As my hand reaches out to touch it Conor rears up, eyes wide, panting.

'It's ok. Conor. It's ok, it's me. I just came to see how you are,' I whisper.

He stares at me, body rigid, hands gripping the duvet. His head jerks in all directions looking around the room, as though it is being pulled by a string.

'Where's the light? There's no air. I can't breathe,'

I rush to open the curtains, and the room becomes brilliant with sunlight so that we both shield our eyes, me looking at him, he turning his head away from me. I wrestle with the warped window frame to jerk open the sash. It knocks against the wood as a tentative breeze enters the stale room.

'There we are, it's ok, here's some air,' I say turning to look at him.

His eyes are fixed on me now, no, on the rectangle of space where the window had been, he is not seeing me. He throws back the duvet and makes to clamber out of the bed.

'Wait, Con, let me help you.'

He cowers away from me when I go to put an arm around him, the thrill of anticipation of physical contact with my husband after all these years destroyed when he pushes me away so hard that I nearly fall backwards. As I regain my balance he collapses back into the bed. I want to touch him but I am wary. Standing in indecision I can hear him muttering. I hold my breath to try and make out what he is saying. I can only discern a few nonsensical words: 'stolen cherries', 'mingling hands', 'wandering water gushes'. I see his eyes, still wide but blank now. Heat radiates from him yet his face remains grey, camouflaged in the duvet as he lies motionless except for his lips, until they too cease moving, remaining parted as he falls back to sleep.

I wait for a while, vacillating between leaving him to slumber and staying to watch over him. It is hard to believe I am looking at my husband, back in our house, back in our bed. The uncertainty of the past seven years is replaced with the uncertainty of the future. I still don't know where he has been and what his return means. Relief that my agony of aloneness has ended, mingles with frustration at this new impasse of uncertainty that has entered my life. With no more sound or movement from him I have to creep away again, as I have done every day since his return.

#

I know Max will be in Winnicott, the bedroom furthest from this one, at the other end of the corridor, door closed and refusing to come out except to take his meals in silence and sneak to the bathroom when he thinks I won't hear him.

Max's capacity to be alone is extraordinary for a seven-year-old child. When he was two years old I found a box of small plastic building bricks in a second-hand shop and bought it, imagining building spaceships and castles with him in a cocoon of togetherness. Max though showed little interest as I pieced the models together, and contempt when we saw that they would never be finished. Instead he squirrelled the multi-coloured bricks away upstairs to his bedroom until one day he just took the box itself after I had abandoned it on the kitchen dresser. Short square towers grew to resemble a bizarrely-coloured moon landscape on the brown of the threadbare carpet. Then I had been pleased, thought that it must be a good sign that Max had found something new to engross him, not noticing that this new absorption was shutting me out.

I encouraged the building at first, buying up any more bricks I came across at jumble sales and in second-hand shops. Over the months the towers became taller, developed into buildings, grew into cities. Max had been slow to walk, late to talk, and when I had tried to encourage him to engage with me by singing, talking to him, looking into his deep-set green eyes, he would always look away, usually down but sometimes just around, anywhere other than at me. Left alone though he populated the cities with characters that only he could see, and they became his companions. I would hear him muttering to them behind the closed door of his bedroom, and witness the abrupt silence that would fall when I entered the room. Now, five years later, my delight has turned to exasperation with his obsession. An obsession that serves only to isolate him further from me.

As I walk down the corridor to Max's bedroom, I have time to rehearse what to say to him. I want to keep it simple, easy, joyous. To help him to understand that his father is back. I want him to show pleasure, to share my excitement.

When I reach his room, I push against the door forcing away the towel he has lain at the foot of it to delay entry. Entering through the narrow gap I ignore that he is ignoring me and sit on the floor beside him. I lean towards him to try and get his attention, knowing that I am competing with the construction of a green multi-storey carpark, fifty bricks tall.

'Max, I have something to tell you.'

He adds another brick.

'Max, please listen to me, stop building for a minute, I need to talk to you.'

Without moving his body Max turns his head to look at me. His face has no expression. It is composed into a perfect blank, dull unblinking eyes, small straight mouth. It unsettles me. I feel like a ghost, present but not present, transparent. A ghost bearing news that will change his life.

With fluttering stomach, I forget what I had prepared and blurt out, 'Max, I need to talk to you about the man asleep in my bedroom.'

There is no change in his countenance. It instils urgency in me. He has to know who Conor is. I have to be the one to tell him

'That man is called Conor, Max, and he is your father. He is the man in the photos and he has come back to us. When he wakes up you can meet him. Would you like that?'

I long for something from Max. A sign that he has heard, that he cares, that he is as keen to get to know Conor as I am. I wait for a reaction, yearn for one. Hand suspended with a green brick in it, Max holds me in a stare of incomprehension until his little boy voice says,

'I don't have a father.'

Closing my eyes, I exhale despair, before mustering myself to explain.

'Of course you do, Max. Everyone has a father. I have told you about yours many times. How he would be back one day. That he loves us and didn't want to leave us. That whatever happened he would find a way back to us. Well now he has Max, and we can be a family. The three of us, you, me, and Conor.'

Max unfolds his hand so that the brick falls. He pushes over the building as he stands up, mouth pursed tight and, I swear, his eyes blazing black. As I look at him from where I kneel on the carpet, he seems so small, and so young, I soften. I want him to feel the happiness that I feel, the hope for a new future. It isn't his fault that all he thought he knew had been thrown into tumult.

'Come on. Come and sit on my lap and I can explain.'

I reach up to lower him down to my level and that's when he punches me. It doesn't hurt of course, but it scares me so that I pull my arm back, a shockwave shivering up my body as I struggle to stand up. Max darts around me and out of the room leaving a swirl of agitated air behind him.

Sinking back to the floor, I sit with the feeling of frustration that is so familiar to me. Always sad at first when it comes, I soon become angry. The rejection, the dismissal, and then the guilt, combine inside before seeping outwards into confusion followed by numbness. He makes me feel useless, a failure, not like a mother. When Max escapes from me, emotionally and often physically, I am left only with defeat. No energy to pursue him, I am left wanting, my conscience being eaten through with a prickling sense of culpability. I should be the one managing these situations, the ones where I try to enthuse him about school, or promise that I love him, and this time, to comfort him through the strange reappearance of the father he never knew. Instead though I question myself, what kind of mother am I?

As the sound of his pounding footsteps recede down the corridor I mute the feelings with relief. I have a reprieve from trying to explain what I cannot explain to a small boy who does not want to know.

Standing to go to the window and watch his tiny powerful body disappear into the woods. I know that as long as Max runs from me and disappears from my sight he disappears from my mind.

He is replaced there by Conor. I picture him lying in the room down the corridor, my room, not caring that I don't know what to tell his son, leaving it all to me. A flash of injustice shoots through me. Enough. I turn and stride out of the room, with satisfying flatfooted stomps towards Bowlby, hoping that Conor can hear me coming.

From the bedroom door I see him, awake but prone, gazing out of the bedroom window from the bed. I stride to its foot and my pain overflows.

'That is your son you can see running away. Running away because I told him that his father is back.'

I want it to hurt, to provoke him into communication. To make him feel like I feel, to understand that I need him to explain. He doesn't.

'Can you hear them? They are calling me to come back,' he says.

'Who is? What do you mean? Come back where?' This is too much. 'Our seven-year-old son is distressed and upset and it is all your fault but you talk nonsense. There is nobody calling you, Conor. Only us, your family. We are calling you. The only person out there is your son, and right now he can't get far enough away. He's running because you are here and he doesn't understand. And you know what? Neither do I. It's time to talk Conor, you have to tell me what is going on.'

When he turns to look at me through rheumy eyes, red-rimmed from sobbing I see in them his hopelessness, a deadening darkness. When he reaches a limp hand towards me, tendrils of panic weave around my insides. A sign? The beginning of learning what has happened? He is trying to speak, maybe the explanation is coming, but now I dread what it will be. With a trembling hand I take hold of his and sit on the bed.

'Conor, darling, please tell me what is going on? Where have you been? I have to know.' The blankness continues to bore into me, until I say, 'I want to share it with you Conor, please tell me.'

At this his body shudders into alertness.

'Do you? Would you like to go there too?'

'Maybe, yes,' I lie. 'Tell me about it and then I can decide.'

I hold my breath, try to still my shaking limbs, wait for answers. Conor is smiling now but with eyes that remain blank and faraway, and I know that he is not here, not with me. Still I wait, hoping, afraid to move, scared to risk dispelling the air of possibility. When his words come they startle me.

'It was the best night of my life.'

I breathe out through my nose, shoulders falling, trying not to let my confusion show in the squeeze of my hand. I am so hoping for more but to ask for it is terrifying. He is smiling as silence drops with the suddenness of a tropical rain shower, and his eyes close. Today will not be the day that I learn where he has been for the past seven years.

As I sit trying to still my mind, the crow that had taken up residence in the tree outside since Conor's return mocks me, laughs at my fruitless wait, caws at me with disdain before flapping its ragged wings to fly in search of its companions. Crows began to roost in the trees lining the driveway when Conor returned, sentry-like, squawking whenever I leave the house. Harbingers of bad luck or goddesses of fortune, depending on who you listen to, their harsh cries send shivers through me every time they herald me leaving the house, so that I hasten out of their sight.

Leaving the bedroom on tiptoes, I turn for one last look at Conor, and to check that the crow is not watching me.

\#

It is a strange prison I inhabit now. It has been six weeks since he returned but he has not left the bedroom nor spoken more than a few words to me. He mumbles the same meaningless phrases over and over again, muttering himself into long restless sleeps. When I creep out of the room and down the corridor, the presence of Conor and Max behind the closed doors of their bedrooms emits a heavy, brooding atmosphere that hurries me down the stairs.

The confines of the house in Conor's absence have expanded into shabby claustrophobia with his return. I wander around it, making meals, changing bedsheets, washing laundry, anything to take my mind off the prolonged agony of knowing no more now about what happened to Conor than I did on the day he disappeared. I miss my PhD studies, abandoned for once and for all, officially, in the year after Conor disappeared. I yearn for that feeling of being immersed in theoretical knowledge that is nothing to do with the reality of my world.

On the day that Max had hit me, I went to search for him after I had left Conor asleep. I looked for him until dusk started to fall. I traced his path into the woods, eyes scanning between the trees, first calling then entreating him with bribes of chocolate, and finally exhorting him to 'Come. Here. Now.'

Max though, is cunning. He waited until I began to blunder my way out of the woods, no doubt watching me as I push away branches that snatch at my face and trip over roots and brambles poking out of the damp earth. As I swiped at the tears that blurred my vision the gloom played tricks on me and I saw figures, darting forms, each one a version of Max, running past me, peering out from behind trees, laughing as my panic took hold. When I emerged from the woods, I saw him, his form lit by the last light of the day as he stood without moving in the middle of the lawn. He was looking at me, utterly still except for the smirk playing on his face. Burning with anger, I slowed to a stride, and walked up to and past him without a word. I did not look back to check that he was following.

I did not speak to him of Conor again until two weeks later, when I explained in flat tones that although Conor was back, I did not know where he had been or why he had returned. I dared not add that I did not know for how long.

I cry a lot, often in muffled sobs but sometimes in loud angry screams with contorted face, dripping nose. Those tears are large and fat, not like the ones that come with the sobs; they trickle down my face, to form streaming rivulets to my chin. Tears are close all the time, waiting just behind my eyes. It's the silences that set them off. The loud silences, the rejecting ones, the angry ones, the despairing ones. They are what inhabit the house instead of the brood of children that I had always dreamed of. When I imagined Conor's return, I thought I had anticipated every possibility of how life would be. How wrong I was. I had not imagined that my husband would be broken when he returned, that he would be pining to be somewhere else with such intensity that it threatened to slice into the very heart that he was breaking.

Yesterday, the eighth week, I named the bedroom that I have moved into. I called it Jung because of the spirals of sadness that I keep revisiting to try and make sense of what is happening. From here I can see the lake, still and calm as always, and the hills behind it rising like an unrolled green canvas that a child has drawn rough lines on with a thick brown crayon. The view still comforts me, and when it is dark, I find my peace in the sound of the distant sea that still rolls in and out despite the craziness in which I am living.

I want to be here, to be necessary so that my two broken men may come to want me to be here, but I long too to be somewhere else where all of this is not happening. I try to escape to the lake where I used to start my days with long languid laps between the reeds that edge it. Now though my strokes are urgent and hurried. The water no longer caresses me but presses against me, makes me breathless as I urge my legs to kick faster and faster. The quick strokes are followed by long footsteps back to the house as my mind fills with anxious thoughts that something bad has happened.

When I get there though it is only my rushed entrance that causes a stir, introducing freshness and light to the dust motes that dance for a moment before settling back down into the dull stillness.

Sometimes I hear a clatter from the main drawing room that Max has recently appropriated by pushing back the only three chairs to the edge of the room to make space for his bricks, and covering the coffee table with drawings of plans for futuristic cities. I imagine him watching the bricks fall and scatter like giant rectangular ants as he demolishes buildings and turns away, disinterested, to move onto the next project. Other times I hear bangs coming from Bowlby, books dropping from Conor's slack hands to splatter onto the floor, rejected, broken-spined.

#

Today is Saturday. I am making a stew. As I peel the carrots to add to the onions and potatoes, bubbling in the tomato sauce, the automaton actions are devoid of the pride of having grown them all myself but serve me well in shutting out the stillness of the occupied house. The silence is broken by the crash of the door knocker. I freeze, peeling knife suspended in my hand. No one ever calls to the house, the rumours about us and the closed gates assure no casual visitors drop in for a cup of tea or come *scoraiochting* in the evening looking for company and gossip. I feel the house's pique at this unusual invasion, and it sends a chill of fear through me. A visitor, so rare and this one so persistent, must only mean something bad.

Placing the knife down and wiping my hands on the front of the green pinafore, I run a hand through the wisps of hair that have escaped my ponytail. I shuffle in my slippers up the staircase to the great hallway, listening for sounds from the bedroom or living room. There is nothing, only my heart thumping. Swinging open the front door I see Mr Murphy. Shiny bald head, slightly sweaty from walking up the driveway, false smile on his round face.

'I'm sorry to call unannounced, Mrs Fairman. I tried to reach you on your mobile but there was no response, and I am keen to talk to you before Max comes back to school on Monday.'

I suppress the sigh and hold one hand with the other to hide the tremble.

'It's quite alright, Mr Murphy,' I lie, 'do come in.'

I lead him across the empty hall, frantic as I try to think where to take him. The kitchen is a mess of carrot, potato, and onion peelings, pungent with the smell of toast burned half an hour before. The chairs around the table are piled with half-folded washing, abandoned since burning breakfast. I can't take him there and I can't take him into the drawing room where Max will stare at him with ill-concealed hatred. It has to be the library, Lacan, now only used by me when the kitchen feels like a cell and the bedroom too close to where Conor is. I walk slowly in front of Mr Murphy with unnatural uprightness and chattering inanely. I must not let him know how strange it is in this house, how unusual to have a visitor, that I have a son playing alone in a room he has shut himself into, and a prodigal husband lying crying in the bed upstairs.

'Here we are, do come in.' I say as we approach Lacan at the back of the hallway. I hasten in ahead of him, needing time to throw open the wooden shutters on the bay window that keep out freshness as well as light. I wave one hand towards a tired overstuffed armchair, that seems to have survived its abandonment without destroying itself. The sunlight pours in and shows up every particle of dust but does nothing to dispel the smell of damp and mustiness. I fix my smile and turn to face him. I am not going to offer him tea, I want this to be over with and to be left to our strange existence. I sit in the non-matching chair across from him, fold my hands on my lap and look Mr Murphy in the eyes.

'What brings you to us today, Mr Murphy? Is all well?'

'Er um, well its Max,' he splutters, 'as I am sure you can guess. You see Max's behaviour has changed over the last few weeks and I am a little concerned.'

I cross my legs and clench them. They carry tightness up my body to my lips.

'I'm afraid that he is scaring the other children with talk of a boogeyman who has come to live with him. He is telling them that the man visits children's bedrooms at night when they are asleep. I am sure you understand, Mrs Fairman, that this is something we have to investigate. I have tried talking to Max, telling him to stop making up stories but he insists that it is true, that he has seen the man. I am worried about what is causing this Mrs Fairman, and I have to ask you, is there any cause for concern about Max's wellbeing that I should be aware of?'

I stare at him as I try to process what he is saying. An ocean heaves and swells in my stomach. He is asking me if there is a man in the house who is a danger to Max. I swallow down the laugh that is twitching around my mouth. The only threat that Conor poses to Max is of ignoring him, not of imposing himself on him. I glance at the ceiling as if I can see Conor through it, comatose in the bed.

'Oh. Well. Mr Murphy, I don't know what to say'

It is true I don't know what to say. For one moment I have the urge to tell him everything that is going on in this house. To share with him my despair and hopelessness with the nightmare that is my life. I can't though. If I start to open that door a flood of terror may drown me. To speak it will make it real, and if it is real I may collapse and never recover. I have to lie, and I have to get rid of him. Assure him and send him away.

'Everything is fine here. Max must be reading a book that is scaring him. You know how much he reads. I'll talk to him, shall I? Try and find out what is going on.' The lies keep coming. 'I'll keep a close eye on him, check him overnight, make sure he is sleeping ok.'

'Is Max here now, Mrs Fairman? Perhaps if I talk to him, he will feel able to say more in his own home than in school.'

Another punch to my stomach. The waves rage into a tsunami.

'Er, no, well yes, he's here,' Mr Murphy will know that Max is not one of the Saturday football-training crowd, down at the pitch, kicking balls around with shouts and hugs for each other, 'but he's asleep. He's got a bit of a cold and I don't want to wake him up.'

This could be the lie that exposes me. If a sound emanates from Winnicott, Mr Murphy will know Max is awake. He will want to talk to him, perhaps ask to look around the house. I must get him out of here.

I glance out of the window for an excuse. Seeing the skies preparing to enter the April showers part of the day I say, 'So sorry, Mr Murphy, but I have to bring in the washing before this rain comes. Was that all you wanted? I can assure you that I will speak to Max and let you know if there is any cause for concern.'

He's not satisfied. He drums his fingers on the chair and looks around the room, studies the books as though seeking out a predator hiding amongst them.

'Weellll, I will leave it with you so, Mrs Fairman, but you must let me know if there is anything we can do to help Max. He is becoming more agitated and I am concerned.' He looks embarrassed as he lowers his head and mutters, 'Not only for him but for the other children.' He gives a half-smile that does nothing but arouse contempt in me. If he only knew what was happening.

I stand up to hasten him away. The walk this time through the hallway to the front door is a quick march, not the hesitant amble of the entry. My ears strain for sounds from within the house, and for once I am grateful for the silence. Shutting the front door too fast, I lean against it. I have to find out if Conor is wandering the house at night, peering in at Max, perhaps peering in at me. The idea makes me shudder.

Chapter 3

Perhaps it is because of my own upbringing that I am such a terrible mother. It's not that I don't feed and care for Max, it's just that I have difficulty loving him. His coldness towards me hurts too much to fight it anymore, and his rejection of me now gives me an excuse to have less and less to do with him.

It has not always been like this. I will never forget the pregnancy, how important it was to protect him as he grew inside me, to nurture him and help him to grow so that when Conor came back we would both be ready to take up the family life that he and I had always dreamed of. Max was going to be the first of our brood of children, all growing up in the embrace of this house, each of whom I would love and be loved by. Being pregnant with Max kept me sane when Conor disappeared. I longed to meet him, to hold him, to be a mother to him.

And then, when he was born, just the two of us in the hospital, no visitors and no family to coo over him and tell me how clever I was, how beautiful he was. I did not care. I held him close, whispered promises to never let him go, told him that we would always have each other, would take care of each other. As he snuffled in my arms I wept over him. I cradled this legacy of Conor and told myself that I had to be strong for both of us until Conor returned.

And I remember our first night together back at the house. We lay together in Bowlby, in the same bed that Conor is lying in now, and I nursed him until he fell asleep, with my finger in the clasp of his tiny, crumpled hand. I tried to stay awake all night so that I could watch over him, be there for him if he woke, and I pictured the life of closeness and love that lay ahead. When I blew out the candle though, and in the darkness sang to him, I could no longer resist falling into a sleep that was the deepest I had since Conor's disappearance. I didn't know it would be the most contented sleep I would have for the rest of Max's childhood.

How soon I broke those promises. I was shocked into wakefulness at daybreak of the very next day by Max's screeching demands. He seemed to need constant feeding, first with my milk which he would sick up in yellow pus-like mucus over all my clothes, and then with formula, that forbidden, disapproved-of substance that seemed to exist only to make mothers feel bad. I think the guilt started then, and it did nothing for Max either. He would spit it out, blowing sloppy raspberries with pursed angry lips. He smeared it with his spindly fingers over his face, his baby-grows, and his filthy stinking nappies when he was able to contort his body to reach them. He screamed when I left him, and he screamed when I went to him. He never settled again, not into my arms where he would squirm and wriggle as though my touch burned him, not into his cot where he would kick his plump legs and wave his short arms like an upturned fly. His colic, his ceaseless crying, his breathless tantrums exhausted me. When he was a baby I used to smell his head, searching for that baby-powder sweetness that would bring us closer. Instead of baby-powder I got vinegar. A preservative. A smell that is not to be shared. It was as though he was no longer mine once he came into this world. My life with Max since that day has been one of running to him, and running away from him, this huge house never feeling large enough to escape him. I know I should feel sympathy for Max, a poor confused child born without a father. I know that what he needs is compassion from me, understanding of his rejection, tolerance of his resentment, but his silences freeze me out and his tantrums drive me away.

Sent to live with Great Aunt Alice when my father sought relief in bottle after bottle of Jameson from depression brought about from losing the love of his life, I was reared in a small, dark house that ran on routine and religion. A kindly older carer, but one who had not wanted nor expected a three-year-old child in her life, Great Aunt Alice raised me according to book-based knowledge, and the church. There was no space for questions or emotions, and little opportunity to learn about love. Instead I turned in on myself, withdrawing to my room to knit, sew, read, write - solitary activities in which I could seek understanding of who I might be. I grew up longing for love and dreaming of becoming the mother I wished I had; the storybook mother who selflessly pours love into her child, fulfilled by watching her grow and thrive.

I struggle to remember my mother now but apparently it was because I looked so like her that my father could not cope with me. I used to spend too long staring into mirrors, wondering if she also resented the straightness of her hair, the shortness of her legs, the millions of tiny freckles on her arms. Now I spend too long wondering if she enjoyed motherhood, enjoyed me, loved me, in the three short years that we had together.

#

The pain of the memories forces me out of bed. I inhale sharply as my legs cramp, stiff from digging a vegetable patch yesterday. Putting on the same gardening clothes, I don't care about the smears of mud and earth and compost because I know I will encounter no one today. No one will notice what I look, or smell, like, and neither do I. Tiredness from a restless night makes me move slowly. My legs protest with every step and the stairs stretch away in a helter-skelter of soreness. It takes an age to reach the kitchen, long enough to make my back ache and my mood grumpy. I slam the filled kettle onto the Aga plate and open the fridge to reach for eggs. When I see there are none, and know that Max will eat nothing else for breakfast, I swing the fridge door closed with more force than it needs before dragging my throbbing body back up to the hallway and out to the henhouse.

Its sharp acrid smell reaches me before I reach the hens. I breathe though my mouth cursing them and their smell for adding to my difficult life. I do not yet know if they will have gifts for me today. It is as though their erratic production has been sent to try me as much as Conor and Max's behaviour does.

Exhaling as I creak my way down onto my knees to lean into the shed and feel around in the slime of wood shavings and manure, I wish that I had remembered gloves. Feeling one then two and a surprise third, alabaster oval, a small quiver of success buzzes in my head. As I pass them out to be held in the grass the angry clucking of the donors dies away. With my intrusion ended I lean back on my knees and look around for the basket I had placed on the ground. It is behind me but that is not what grabs my attention.

In the last week Conor has taken to reciting over and over again 'The Stolen Child' by Yeats. Sometimes he mutters it under his breath, skipping some words and emphasising others. Other times he roars out the lines, flailing his arms and shouting them towards the window. I have heard the words so often now that I have come to know them all. Whenever I enter his bedroom I expect to hear them, for them to be what holds his attention and not me. Now as I sit on the damp grass and massage my aching knees and calves, I let them wash over me.

'*Away with us he's going,*
'*The solemn-eyed:*
He'll hear no more the lowing
Of the calves on the warm hillside'

As I knead my muscles it occurs to me that I can make out the words clearly. The henhouse is below the bedroom window, once a source of laughing complaint, but if Conor is in bed the sound would not carry this far. I look up, expecting to see him leaning out, calling the words out to the hills, but he is not there. I kneel more upright, confused. Where is he that I can hear him so well?

'Or the kettle on the hob
Sing peace into his breast'

I look around trying to locate him. Has he left the bedroom at last? The kitchen garden is behind me, its neat rows of polytunnels and raised beds marching towards the dilapidated stables. Conor is not there. Now the sound of the poem ebbs and flows with the wind.

'Or see the brown mice bob
Round and round the oatmeal chest'

I am on my feet. I turn around in circles looking across the expanse of lawn and back towards the house. I cannot see him anywhere as the words continue to sing in the wind.

'Come away O human child'

I can understand why Conor gains comfort from this poem. It speaks of another world, a world to be whisked away to, where happiness can be found and sadness left behind. With a jolt I feel scared. The poem holds promises for Conor, offers him something not available to him here. I know the ending of it too. My lips feel dry and my throat flutters as panic rises. Where is he? What is he doing?

Is he in the stables? I begin to run towards them, and then come to a sudden stop as I remember the next lines

'To the waters and the wild'

The lake! Turning on my heels, skidding in the mud I dash towards the water. Pushing through its overgrown edges to find my familiar track to the water, I see him waist deep, wading out to the centre of the lake. The low waves churn as he pushes through the reeds shouting out the final lines.

'With a faery, hand in hand.'

He has Max. He is gripping his hand and pulling him through the grey-blue water. Max is compliant, silent, his other hand stretched out in front of him out as the depth of the water increases, rising up to his neck. Terror takes over me. I cannot reach them in time by swimming out.

'Conor, Conor, stop, what are you doing?' I yell.

The pair keep moving, I see Max spit out a dribble of water as it splashes into his mouth.

'Stop, Conor, come back. Max make him stop.'

I am helpless on the bank of the lake, now understanding how Conor has interpreted the poem. I start pulling off my wellington boots as he turns to me and calls out the final line.

'*For the world's more full of weeping than he can understand.*' I'm saving him Marianne, I'm saving both of us. We will be happy. He will never know the sadness of this world. I am taking him back.'

My voice, when I find it, is high pitched, thin, weak, hardly reaching across the stretch of churning liquid between us.

'He has known the sadness already, Conor, you can give him happiness by living. By being with us. By being the father to him you always wanted to be.'

It's enough to make Conor hesitate. I see him stop, turn to look at Max. I stride into the water, trying to find strength in my voice, the best tool I have to stop this happening. The crows are circling, cawing their mockery, competing with my words. It is as though they are encouraging Conor to complete his plan. He looks up at them as I wade fast through the lake trying to gain enough depth to start swimming. I thrust forward using my arms to push my body.

Conor lets go of Max as he slips on unseen silt and I scream over the crows, 'Come back, Max, come on, start swimming back. Move as fast as you can.'

Conor turns with awkwardness in the water to grab at Max with determination. I think he is going to force Max's head under the water. I know now that his endless reciting of the poem over the last weeks has been him making this plan. He longs for Max to come to the other world with him, the world without weeping that he longs to return to.

'Don't, Conor, please don't'

It is useless. He pays me no attention, looks straight ahead and pushes against the power of the water to take Max away with him. My entreaties are nothing.

A wind whips up, bites at my face as I move forward in the thick treacle. Conor snatches over and over at Max who is trying to thrust his way back towards me. He is shouting, entreating him to stay with him but Max ploughs on. Finally, in deep enough water I take in a lungful of air and dive, feeling the freezing water close over my head, shutting out the nightmare playing out above me. Everything slows down in the silent murky world underwater and I have no idea of what I will find when I surface again. In a masochistic distraction it flashes through my head to never emerge, to stay in the silence until I lose all control of myself. My body takes over though and forces me upwards, panting and gasping. I am facing the shore and as a stab of fear penetrates me, I turn on the spot until I see them again.

Max is closer to me than to Conor now, and Conor is watching him with desolation etched into every crevice of his gaunt face.

'Good boy, come on, Max, keep going,' I call out.

Max reaches me but evades my clumsy attempt to grab him and swims past as though I am not there. Only Conor is in front of me now, still staring at Max, arms still stretching for him, but in defeat.

'Your turn, Conor, come on, come back this way, Max will be safe on the shore in a minute.'

My voice attracts his attention, and his eyes, those emerald green eyes, move from Max to me. He looks at me with curiosity, not knowing who I am. His head cocks to one side, tendrils of wet hair clinging to the side of his face. I shout to encourage him again and again until he snaps into the present and begins to wade through the water towards me.

I stay where I am, treading water with one arm held out to him. I compose my face into a false calm as I beckon him on. Curious moorhens watch from a safe distance and a Canada goose takes off in startled flight. When Conor is close enough for me to feel the spittle from his puffs of exertion hit my face, I snatch his hand and without a word, lead the two of us towards the bank where we both put our feet down and feel them sink into the lake bottom. As we stand in water up to our thighs I put my arms around him, and hear him whisper. 'He called me Dad, Marianne, I'm his father.'

'Of course you are,' I reply.

A tremor of excitement ripples through me as my insides melt and feel as wet as my wrinkling skin. Hearing Max call him Dad was what stopped the tragedy that was so close. Perhaps this is the breakthrough he needed.

#

Conor and Max had not developed any relationship at all in the past six weeks. Max maintained his disinterest in Conor, indifferent to the sounds of his shouting and crying, and Conor hid away in the bedroom. Yet sometimes I find Max sitting in the corridor outside the bedroom listening to Conor moaning and muttering. I hear him creeping around at night, sometimes creaking open the door to Conor's room. Once he asked me if Conor is staying forever now. Often, he rages at me, casting blame for allowing this man to bring disruption to our lives.

I know Max is jealous of the attention I give Conor. I have been at Conor's beck and call since his return, anticipating his moods, answering his summons, hoping for some signs of recovery. Max is right in feeling he is second in my attention, a position he has not been used to. His behaviour at school has worsened, making his continuing attendance there tenuous, and my guilt at not being of help to either my husband or my son has grown. I am short and terse with him when I should be open and loving. Max sees Conor as a barrier to his relationship with me, and I see him as a barrier to Conor's recovery.

Today though the stakes have upped. Conor has become a danger, to himself and to Max. It was awkward to manipulate Conor's limp body back to the house, but I had wrapped myself around him, gripping whatever part of him that I could. We were one as we mounted the stairs to the bathroom, and I seated him on the floor of the shower. Afterwards, I dried him as best I could with our largest cardboard-textured towel and he revived a little, able to stand and take small pigeon footsteps to the bedroom. Once there he sank onto the bed and fell asleep with not a word having passed between us.

As he slept, it soothed me to tidy and clean the room. Working in the stale and stagnant space, I removed the used coffee-ringed cups and crumb-filled plates atop the bedside cabinets, tidied the books strewn beside and under the bed, and took away the worn pyjamas piling up in the corner. With the debris cleared, I filled a bowl with soapy water and washed and wiped every part of the room, swiping at cobwebs on the high ceiling, rubbing the fingerprints from the window frame, reaching behind the wardrobe with a duster. I worked in a frenzy until the room felt, and smelt, fresh. It could be anybody's bedroom, cleaned and tidied whilst an exhausted husband slept off the day's exertions in it. Except that it was daytime, and his exertions had been to attempt to kill himself and his son.

Worn out I stand to look at Conor. He could almost be the Conor I remember now, older of course with his newly washed, slightly-too-long-for-his-age hair draped around his face, its red sheen showing through the grey hairs. The face it frames is at rest, the tension morphed into a smooth paleness. maybe dreaming of our fully restored house and happy gang of children. He looks like he is at peace for the first time since he returned. It is hard to understand that this is the same man who planned to kill our child.

I had tried so hard to care for him, to give him comfort, to enable space and time for his recovery. I had put myself and Max to one side but now I wonder if this had been the wrong thing to do. Perhaps I should have worked harder to bring him close to Max. Maybe by standing between them I had only worsened his despair at being back. Should I have done more to let them find their way back to each other? Could I have helped to awaken the loving Conor who could be nurtured into a new life as Max's father? Would that have prevented the near-tragedy that had so nearly engulfed us? And now? Can I overlook what he tried to do? Trust him again? Leave him alone? Leave him with Max? The turmoil in my mind is ceaseless as I watch. Conor's breathing is deep and regular, in contrast to mine, which speeds up as awful possibilities of what might have happened invade my mind. Next time he reaches out to take himself and Max to that world he longs for, I may not be there to keep him in this one.

#

When I rouse myself to leave the bedroom, sure that Conor will sleep for hours, I go to find Max. He is in the drawing room and I push open the double doors without knocking. He brushes at his eyes before looking up at me from the floor where he is sitting amongst a pile of bricks. He has destroyed his city and he sits in its ruins like an abandoned child in a war zone. Saying nothing I cross the floor and kneel down in front of him, looking into his eyes.

'Are you ok, Max?'

'I'm fine, Mum,' he replies, voice wavering.

I reach out with both arms, and he sinks into them. I am flooded with pleasure. My boy is letting me hold him, be with him, be there for him. He called me Mum. The pleasure hurts as much as it pleases me. To hold Max like this is an act so unusual that I know he must be in turmoil to allow it. I want to stay like this forever, loving and protecting my poor, confused son.

When he pushes me away he says in a gruff voice, 'I told you we shouldn't have allowed him back didn't I?'

I can only say, 'He doesn't know what he is doing, Max. he can't help himself. He loves you and that is what he thought he was showing you.'

'Do you love me, Mum?'

His words floor me. Never has he asked me this question, and with guilt, I cannot remember the last time I told him that I did.

'I love you completely, Max. Never doubt it. My love for you is huge and I do everything I can to show you that.'

It feels so strange to be saying this out loud. I silence the voices in my head that query the words I am saying. I do love him. I do love him. I do love him.

At that moment I hear a shout from the bedroom. It is loud and anguished, a howl. I look at Max and lean to kiss him. He turns his head away and picks up a brick. I push myself up from the floor, and my leaden legs carry me out the door and up the stairs.

In the bedroom Conor is sitting up in bed, hair now sticking up, a sheen of sweat over his face. He looks at me with terror in his eyes. I see flashes of fear as his hands scrabble with each other over the duvet. I rush over to hold him and feel his body stiffen. He makes a feeble attempt to push me away but within seconds collapses and clutches me to him with a grip that speaks only of desperation. His head sinks to my chest, sobbing, with body shaking. We half-sit, half-lie there, his body clammy, dampening his tee-shirt and sending odorous wisps of fear around me and into the room. I am alert, unsure. If I try to move, he grabs me closer to him, crying out with neediness.

'I am his father,' he whispers.

I can only hold him tighter in the thick silence that follows.

When darkness slinks in an hour later, we are tumbled together on top of the crumpled duvet. I shove it away with my feet, my shoes thumping onto the floorboards as we wriggle back together. I feel my wedding ring slip off, and hear it roll away.

#

The next day Conor is different. When I bring in a boiled egg and toast he ignores the offerings and starts talking. Halting at first but soon becoming fast and breathless, his words fall over each other as he uses the eloquence he always had to paint a world of beauty, of appreciation, of a community where all members work together for food and the preservation of nature. A world with members drawn from everywhere, and where difference makes no difference. He tells me that he spent one glorious night there and on waking up and finding himself back in this world seven years later he wants only to return to that one. I press him for more information, trying to make sense of what he is telling me. I ask him where this place is, and how he got there. He talks of following a light on the way home from the pub and finding himself in a castle, dazzling with light emanating from thousands of fireflies and exaggerated by the costumes covered in sparkling jewels worn by hundreds of revellers. He tells me about the unending music that compelled him to dance, and of being welcomed and encouraged by the other partygoers to join them.

Conor's description is so vivid that I find it easy to imagine this place. A place of light and joy, celebration and happiness. As he talks, I can almost hear the music on the breeze coming through the window, and I think I can see dots of light flitting about the sparsely furnished bedroom. I have to remind myself that this makes no sense. There is no place that I know of that fits this description. Celebrations in pubs and clubs for GAA or Debs end of school graduation ceremonies, yes, but no castle glowing with light that can be seen from miles away as he describes.

It is so real to him though. I look at Conor as he talks on, in English, no more Gaelic. His face is glowing as he recalls his experience, his eyes are lit as if the fireflies have taken up residence there, and shine into the room. As his arms paint shapes in the air to enrich what he is saying I feel a warmth creeping through me. His animation is a sign of life, of Conor, of a return to me. He is released from the capsule that has held him in silence and sadness since he returned. My storm of joy and bewilderment will have to be dealt with later despite my head and my heart whirling.

I have a million questions but am afraid to ask them. What sort of light did he see? How did it entice him to follow? Why does it feel like one night when it was seven years? What else happened in that time? None of this is sensible, but I am torn between revelling in his communication and fearing to cast doubt on it. As he talks on and on I don't want him to stop, ever. I don't care what he is saying. For now.

With no warning though he does stop speaking. Staring out of the window the flicker in his eyes dies and they cloud once again. Wrinkles appear on his forehead as he remembers something. Something that he doesn't want to remember. I wait, afraid to move, afraid to breathe. I want to know.

When he turns his head to look at me I see the blackness of despair fall on him again. The spell he has woven is broken and I know that I won't learn any more today. Something is distressing him, but he retreats back into silence, unable to tell me. Is he protecting himself or me? Conor is back in this world, the one he now finds so hard to be in, and he hides from it by lying back down on the crumpled, sweat-stained sheets and closes his eyes. I breathe again but now in quiet exasperation. He is lost to me again. I slide out of the bed, pull the duvet over him and sit watching as he falls into slumber of hopelessness.

For the rest of that day I am drained. Contaminated by Conor's despair, and my own helplessness to help him, my body gives up on me and I slump in an armchair unable to even lift my hand to move the hair from my face. Today I have been petrified into inertia, panicked into franticness, and dashed down into despondence. The rollercoaster has left me flooded with powerlessness. My cracked heart knows that what we had, what we wanted, what we began to create, is not enough for Conor and now he is a threat. Deep down I know I have lost him.

Chapter 4

The awful event of yesterday exhausted all three of us but as Max and Conor sleep through this morning I rise at the same time as I always do. I plod through the gloom of the house as dawn breaks, down the stairs to the kitchen where my hands mechanically reach for the kettle. The calmness of my movements betrays the whirring of my mind. My husband tried to kill my son. There was nearly a murder-suicide in my home. I nearly didn't get to the water in time to stop it. I can still smell its tang as the lake resisted my desperate journey across it. I can see Conor's blank determined face as Max flails in the water, and I can feel the searing panic that rose through me as events unfolded in slow motion.

My feet falter on the cold tiles of the kitchen floor, even as my arms lift the kettle to pour boiling water over the teabag. I don't see Conor's photo this morning as I hold the cup with both hands to calm my shaking and think through what to do. Doing nothing is tempting. I want to deny what happened, to give in to believing that we can carry on with another day, suppressing anxiety, pretending things can still get better. I know though that I have not done enough to help Conor and that is why we have come to this. The awful possibility that I will never be able to do enough, that I will never be enough, takes up residence in my head and I know that I have to rise above the pain to save my son, even if it means giving up Conor.

#

The riverside village became a thriving market town with the upgrade of the one entry road from the city. Along that road thundered lorries full of rarely-seen produce such as pineapples and melons, coachloads of tourists, and expensive cars driven by factory owners seeking profitable opportunity on the hitherto unspoilt riverbanks. Now, it's neat pastel-coloured rows of houses are dominated by modern estates built into the hills above them, the narrow roads built for donkey and cart clog with motorised traffic, and the pavements, only two slabs wide, teem with young families, hippies, and tourists.

When the town's tourist potential was recognised, money was lavished on smartening the high street. Not wanting to shake off its roots as a rural outback serving farmers and tradesmen, its boutiques, and coffee shops nestle alongside pubs in front rooms of houses, and hardware stores selling farm equipment. The weekly cattle mart moved to the outskirts of the town, next door to the fish factory, to make space for car parking and a weekly Country Market where everything from eggs, to jam, to chickens, and clothes from India can be bought throughout the year.

When we first bought the house, Conor and I liked to wander the town's narrow streets, discovering hidden alleyways and river walks. We imagined the history of the large families who once were the town's sole inhabitants, sustaining themselves as fishermen, shopkeepers, and pub owners. People we met were friendly and welcoming, even more so when they learnt that we had bought the 'big house' on the town's outskirts and we shared with them our delight in planning its restoration.

'You're brave ones to take on that house.'

'You've some work to do there.'

It was after Conor disappeared that the feeling of being welcome changed. Of course, the mystery that surrounded his disappearance was 'solved' by the gossips, the idle, and the pure malicious in the town: he had another family, he had returned to his hometown, he had gone abroad to find work, he could no longer stand being with me, he couldn't take the abuse, the blows to his pride, the lack of consideration, the misery, the distress that I must have caused. The mystery though became less and less mysterious until 'It was no wonder he escaped, she drove him to it' became its solution. Interest waned and moved on. When old Mary O Reilly had all her windows double glazed the town's sleuths went back to work, determining that 'she must have come into money'.

I was never present to hear the 'other' stories of disappearances, the stories told around living-room fires and, in whispers, at the bar: of little Cian Murphy, the young boy assumed to have been washed away by a freak wave one night when he had snuck out of his bedroom; of young Sinead O Driscoll, the unmarried daughter of the local publican, discovered two years later living in Galway with a woman; and of PJ O Brien, the aged father of poor Patrick, believed to have stumbled into the lake trying to find his way home from calving one night. No bodies and no proof but the only explanations for otherwise unexplainable disappearances. I knew about them though. Similar tales had weaved around the small village I had grown up in and I had no doubt that similar explanations about Conor will have joined the ranks.

On the night Conor disappeared the guards took some practical steps: questions were asked, phone calls made, and woods, lake, and fields searched. Nothing. At my insistence posters were drawn up and pinned to lampposts and trees. I rang the hospitals, scoured the town, the road, and eventually, the garden of the house. When I was in the house I could not rest, jumping at the shadows that resided there and in my head. They never stopped teasing, taunting, and provoking me. Where is he? Why has he gone?

I became aware of gossip about me on one of my first outings with Max in his pram. One morning, when he was three weeks old, I emerged from the house, hair wild and unkempt, pregnancy weight hanging heavy, eyes blinking at the daylight after the gloom of where we had been holed up for weeks. Until then Max and I had remained hidden away, surviving on late night dashes to the petrol station to scoop up bare essentials with head down, muttering 'thanks a million' to the disinterested teenager landed with the night shift.

Out of supplies again I had mustered up enough energy to thrust him into the tattered second-hand pushchair, and down the drive. I felt brave to leave the house in daylight and risk meeting people. I hadn't been brave during my pregnancy - only pragmatic - suppressing panic and despair to focus on growing Conor's baby in the best possible way. I succeeded. Max was the perfect baby in shape and temperament on the day he was born. Subservient to the prods and pokes that announce arrival into this world, feeding well before falling into a slumber that soothed the very air around him. The nurses at the hospital complimented me on the calmness with which he awoke, gurgling and searching for milk.

'What a dote. You'll have no trouble with him,' said the midwife who hours earlier told me that Max would be the fiftieth baby she had helped into the world.

I smiled as I prepared to take him home.

Those screams as he awoke on our first morning at home jarred, a painful contrast to the gentle gurgling of the night before. Harsh, demanding cries that coursed through my head then, and for months after. From then on I tried so hard to attend to him, feed him, soothe him, to understand what he wanted, but nothing was ever right. I gave him everything I could until I had nothing left to give. His relentless cries for satiation tortured me. If they were not searing me, the silences teased me, dared me to relax, mocked me when I did. When the house was silent I paced it, when Max screamed I went to him, trying to anticipate what he might want, never getting it right. Slowly Max became a raging monster who controlled me and imprisoned me in the house, and I became a failure as a mother.

Max started wriggling and screaming from the minute I put him in the pram. His tiny scrunched up face red with the effort of trying to fight his way out of my arms, he kicked at the struts even after I succeeded in strapping him in. I could hardly push it in a straight line because of his flailing, not a problem down the long driveway but harder on the narrow pavements of the town. That first time people stepped out of the way with a tut-tut or a sympathetic smile if we bashed their ankles. Inside the shops they were less forgiving as his screams bounced off the shelves, ricocheted from the freezers and pierced customers' ears. Then he was quiet. With relief I scanned the shelves but turning to place the washing-up liquid in the pram's hood I saw his red face turning blue. He was holding his breath with the concentration of a knowing victor. I fled the shop, only realising when I got home that the unpaid for washing-up liquid was still in the pram.

The next time, forced out of the house by a temporary power cut preventing me from being able to sterilise his bottles, I waited until Max had worn himself into a tantrum-induced sleep before laying him into the pram to wheel it down the drive, dreading that every bump might wake him. His exhaustion lasted for ten minutes of the forty that we were out. I saw eyerolls that spoke of sympathy or annoyance as I manoeuvred my pushchair filled with a screeching monster up the steep step into Cronin's grocery store, and saw women in the queue whispering to each other, pointing at me with failed furtiveness. I melted for an instant when Mrs Barry bustled up to me to place a hand on my shoulder and say, 'My dear, I was so sorry to hear.' I allowed myself to absorb longed-for sympathy, but before the relaxation had time to dissolve through my body her next words hardened the softness.

'Some men just can't handle their women being pregnant. It's not your fault you picked a wrong 'un love.'

As she waddled out of the shop and towards the church with a smirk that showed how pleased with herself she felt, all I could see was Conor smiling up at me on our first night in our new house and telling me how much he wanted us to have a child. She was right in one respect, it was not my fault, but she was so wrong in labelling sweet, caring Conor as a 'wrong 'un'.

Learning fast how people had formed their judgements, I anticipate their words before I hear them now.

'That's the one who drove her husband away when she was pregnant.'

'He had to get away you know – she was driving him crazy'

They come most often from people in queues, whiling away their time as they wait their turn. First, they speak with their eyes, staring before turning away with tight lips. Then they whisper loud enough for everyone to hear, a smile playing on their faces. I ignore them, stand in my place with face fixed, looking straight ahead. I know even this provides fodder for the rumour mill; unfriendly, aggressive, sour, beyond help.

It has become quite easy to avoid too many of these encounters. The kitchen garden now produces vegetables all year round and the orchard gives us apples and pears in Summer. Our first hen, Betsy, has been joined by three others and a rooster. Poppy the goat is a good milker, and a good listener, offering a silky listening ear with little complaint as I squeeze her udder and cajole her to give up nutritious liquid. Occasionally I creep into the Saturday market to purchase a rabbit for the pot, taking the opportunity to snatch up a few tins of baked beans and packets of pasta from the 'cheaper' supermarket next door. I brave the gauntlet of looks and whispers, keeping my head down, and letting the whispers drift away over me. I tell myself that I am not the person they think I am, that Conor is not the man they think he is. I pretend they are talking about someone else when they talk of abandonment and driving loving husbands away.

#

Today, when Max and I reach the town, small waves in my stomach ripple as I negotiate the narrow pavements. He is no longer in a pram of course and his lithe seven-year-old's body keeps step with mine whilst at the same time managing to appear as though he is not walking with me. With my head down to avoid any eye contact, I make for the supermarket that I know has a noticeboard for customer advertisements. Nobody bothers me as I rustle through the layers of paper, from the small and scrappy handwritten to A4 sized photos of cute kittens and puppies for sale. Leaning over trolleys of goods left there whilst their owners lunch in the adjacent café I collect details of acupuncturists, psychotherapists, yoga teachers and a Chinese herbalist.

Next stop is the doctor's surgery. This is more daunting. There will be bored and nosey patients waiting in the small room where the Reception desk is, delighted to be distracted by my entry.

Pushing open the glass door with both hands, the place seems to shrink. I tower over the six or seven seated men and women as I clump towards the desk, Max trailing behind me. Its low height forces me to lean forward to speak as quietly as I can to the bespectacled woman who glares at me from the depths behind it. It is as though I am intruding on her time, and that her patience is further tested when I stand, hesitating, over her.

'Yes? Can I help you? Do you have an appointment?' she barks.

Staring at her I managed to stutter, 'No, but I have a query,'

We look at each other, she waiting whilst tapping her pencil against the telephone she had been about to pick up, me reddening and clammy beneath the anorak that is too warm for the over-heated room. The air of expectation behind me infiltrates the pores of my skin and I am annoyed at myself that my hands are trembling. I lower them out of sight of the glaring receptionist.

'Can you tell me your opening hours?' I ask,

I hate myself for my cowardice. Too aware of the listening ears I cannot bear to admit my need for help with Conor. Fumbling in my mind for a gracious exit the question had stumbled out.

Raising her eyebrows so that her magnified eyes are wide the woman suppresses a sigh and nods her head to a sign by the door. I nearly trip over my own feet as I turn to walk over to it past a row of curious onlookers sitting in silence. Beneath the laminated sign with 'Opening Hours' written above numbers that blur in front of me, are tatty posters about mindfulness and meditation classes, help for 'mental health' offered by the surgery. I am pleased of the excuse to pull out my notebook in front of the watching eyes of the waiting patients.

Leaving the stifling atmosphere, I go to the internet café where booths offer safe places to hide. I dive into one and take a seat after depositing Max in front of a computer in the adjacent booth. I smile with gratitude when the young, bearded hipster approaches me looking tired and disinterested.

'Do you wanna' drink?' he drawls.

Composure restored I request a coffee for me and a hot chocolate for Max, and begin to search.

Typing in 'mental health support services' flashes up a daunting screed of information; names, clinics, support groups, spanning page after page. Help is available for depression, psychosis, hearing voices, anxiety, wellbeing. At the click of a button I find lists of symptoms that seem to describe Conor in every example. Whatever hypochondria on behalf of someone else is, I develop it as I read through. I don't know whether he has depression, is psychotic, suffers excessive anxiety, is dissociated, hears voices. He fits all of these. I slump in the swivel chair one finger pressing the forward arrow on the keyboard over and over without my brain taking in what appears. It is only when I am jolted back by the hipster teenager coming to take away my empty cup that I go back to the first page and write down the details of the first five services. At the counter we exchange money without a word, his attention back to his mobile phone before I have left the shop.

#

My list covers a sheet of A4 but it all merges into a blank page out of which pop upbeat positive words such as 'positivity', 'happiness', 'courage'. None of it is helpful in deciding what might be best for Conor.

When I tell Conor I want us to get some help his answer does not surprise me.

'No one here can help me. The only people who can are in another world that has cast me out for being human.'

He has fixated on the notion of having been to another world and when he does speak it is only to tell of his longing to return to it. The idea that is it so hard for him to be human and back with his family annoys and desolates me. How ridiculous it is that I am trying to help him to accept who he is, when he rejects the fundamental starting point. How sad to think that the challenge that lies ahead for him lies in being who he is. I decide to start with the idea of using his body to get back in touch with himself, and sign him up for a yoga programme.

#

I must prepare both Conor and Max for the first visit.

'Come on, Conor, let's have a shower.'

He is silent and compliant as I put my arm around his shoulder to make the journey across the landing to the bathroom. As he sits on a stool in the shower, I wipe a flannel over his body. I notice the moles that were there before he left, and the new wrinkles that were not. I mourn his wasted muscles, remembering how easily he used to bound around the house, moving furniture and painting walls.

He shows no emotion when I dress him in his old grey tracksuit and dirty white trainers, the hooded top and baggy trousers hanging off his thin frame. His damp hair clings around his face and he does nothing to push it back only staring ahead from those now flat and faded emerald green eyes.

Negotiating the stairs challenges both of us. He tells me he feels giddy and gives whimpers of fear as his feet search for each creaking step. His weight on me, slight though it is, threatens to unbalance me with each jerk. After what feels like hours, we reach the front door. I can feel the heat in my body increasing as I start to worry about the journey. Max waits without a word, watching us, mouth pursed, book in hand.

When I open the door and the freshness of the garden blows in with a gust of rain-scented air, Conor gasps and turns away. It has been weeks since he has been outside his bedroom, and he has never been outside the house since his return.

'Come on Conor, let's do this.' I urge.

He looks at me for the first time since this venture began.

'Are we going back? Are you taking me there?' he asks.

I mumble an ambivalent answer, not exactly lying but not telling him where we are going either, and manage to persuade him to get into the car. Max sits in the back, head bowed, reading his book intently, apparently oblivious to this grown man being treated like a toddler.

The journey is silent. Conor clings to the handle above the passenger door, knuckles white and body rigid, scared of the movement of the car. I grip the steering wheel, staring at the grey river of road that may be the beginning of Conor's journey back to us.

#

Conor and I are lost in the empty, high-vaulted room. White muslin curtain billow against the smoky tinted glass frontage giving glimpses of the high street outside where I can see Max seated in the car. The occasional chatter and laughter from people passing seems invasive in this peaceful space.

'Hi, I'm Jeff, you must be Conor.'

The tall, lean man beams as he approaches us holding out a slender, tanned hand. My stomach lurches with dread as I anticipate Conor's response.

Staring at Jeff and then around the cavernous space, the rest of Conor's body remains motionless. I press a hand on his back, willing him to make some acknowledgement of Jeff but when he stumbles with fright at my touch I step backwards, face flushed.

Jeff had assured me by phone a couple of days earlier that he could work with Conor. He told me that he had been successful in helping people with all kinds of conditions to reconnect with their minds by learning to be in touch with their bodies. His demeanour on the phone, and now here in person, is one of acceptance, and kindles a small flame of hope. I cannot wait to leave Conor alone with him, to hand him over.

Back at the car, I see as I approach that Max has not lifted his head from the book he is reading in the backseat. I swerve so that my feet now take me to a coffee shop a few doors down. Max won't notice I have not returned until he reaches the book's end.

#

I have no idea how that first yoga session went. When I returned to collect Conor, Jeff was all smiles and comforting words.

'We made a great start. With work, he'll be fine.'

I wanted to accept the words, to believe them, and my face arranged itself into a thankful smile, but the vacant stare on Conor's face was still there as I led him out into the bustle of the street and guided him into the car.

It marked the beginning of weeks of silent journeys to meet with welcoming strangers. I lead Conor into living rooms, studios, and consulting rooms for assessments, classes, and sessions. On the days of appointments, I help him wash and dress, murmuring encouraging words. He makes no response, lifts his arms on request, slips feet into fresh socks and newly cleaned trainers, acquiesces to having his long hair brushed back into a pony tail and the shoelaces on his trainers tied. As we drive along empty country roads to remote houses and small villages, I try to prepare him, hoping for some uplift in his motivation, wanting comfort that I am doing the right thing for him.

When Max allows it, I sit outside the offices or watch through windows into studios. I hear only quiet muttering or see Conor bend and stretch in accordance with directions from lean and flexible instructors. Back at the house I congratulate him, question him, and brew up foul-smelling teas which he drinks without complaint and only the occasional wince.

After six months there is little change. True he has not attempted suicide again, nor threatened Max, and does sometimes leave the bedroom. I feel guilty every time I suggest he may want to go back up to it, knowing that it is more for me than for him. I feel his presence everywhere, but if I try to speak to him, he drops his head and shuffles away with quick short steps, repelling and rejecting me. In the next moment he pursues me, calling around the house, and tugging at my sleeve when he finds me. He clings to me, begs me to understand what he is pining for, until eventually he withdraws back into his misery. These days are impossible. My growing guilt at wishing he would stay confined to the bedroom gnaws at me, but his presence drains and threatens to infect me with his despair, so I encourage him to sleep. He rarely argues, Pleased, I tell myself, to shut out the reality that he cannot bear to be part of.

Sometimes when I sit with him, he clutches me to him, declaring that he can't live here without me, wants me to be at the bedside when he wakes, petrified not of sleep but of waking. He reaches out for me, wraps himself around me, whimpering in sadness at the realisation once again that he is here. Once I welcomed this, saw it as an opportunity, now though, I have to struggle not to recoil from him. It is not me he is reaching for but something from me that I cannot give. It hurts too much to risk an angry rejection of my attempts to soothe him. It is easier to let his pleas bounce off me, his hands to clasp cold stone instead of warm flesh. Occasionally he wanders the garden, dismissing my company, avoiding Max's. He mutters as he shuffles around, breaking down into sobs of anguish, calling out into the wind. Sometimes we used to cry together, but more and more often now, we cry apart.

The new unease in our house drives me out of it daily. The suffocating silence is a directive to me to leave and whenever I can slip away I do. I wander the gardens, relishing its contrasts of soft green and woody brown. I feel safe and secluded in my isolation as I stroll. The further I wander from the house the more protected I feel. Unseen sentries guard me as I lean towards the earth to examine new shoots, reach upwards to pick dead leaves to cast my cares with them to the ground. Sometimes I think I hear snatches of laughter in the air, feel a consoling pat on my shoulder, I think I see a flitting light. The stories of the house having been built on fairy ground flits back into my mind at these times, but I don't feel frightened, only cosseted.

It is unusual for me to walk in the woods, preferring more often to stay in the light-filled openness of the meadows and fields, wandering down to the lake and back up around the orchard but today I am drawn there. I see flashes of green amongst the trees and hear tinkling sounds, like water, trickling through it. I have come out to walk after a sharp heavy rain shower. Perhaps a new gully has formed on the woody floor. My wellington-shod feet plunge step by step through puddles of oozing black mud. I like to fight the pull of the swamp with the dry comfort of my boots. A wispy mist swoops and swirls in front of me so that my face feels warm and wet. 'Tis a soft day,' I think, hearing birds trilling to each other across grey mist-shrouded sky. I wonder why they sing. Is it their freedom that makes them so happy?

The woods are dark, watery sun stabbing the gloom. The mist flounces in front of me, catching light shafts that illuminate twists of smoky air. As I advance deeper in through the tall leaning pines, stepping with care over gorse, treading down nettles, the smell of wood, damp and pungent, gets stronger. Its odour weaves around me, encases me as my feet start to feel heavier. The effort to move becomes harder. I feel sleepy. I trip over a tree root, and afterwards, upright again, I stand still and close my eyes. It is as though the wood is holding its breath and I realise the birds have fallen silent. There is no space for sunlight anymore. The wood's canopy obscures the sky and forms a sheltering roof. I am aware only of bark-strewn ground, soft and wet beneath my feet, and of protective tree trunks surrounding me. I lower myself to the ground and give into my urge to lie down, close my eyes, let the wood wrap itself around me. It exhales its sweet-scented breath over me, and I breathe in deeply though my nose. I feel cared for, at one with this wood. I want to stay here forever. Behind closed eyes I see tiny sprites dancing in little flashes of light. I feel my skin being caressed and I remember Conor as he used to be, the feelings of love and joy that we had. I am happy and at peace. I want to sleep, never to wake.

#

The shrill squawk of a crow stirs me into abrupt wakefulness. The woods awaken too, birds chatter in alarm, swooping away in packs, beautiful and panicked. Leaves rustle with irritation and branches shake off the crows taking up sentry on them. There is a new light now, a twilight that tells me I must have lain here for hours. Jumping up I feel the mud oozing higher up my legs than before, sucking, gurgling and releasing bubbles of stagnant stinking air. I have lost my bearings and fear takes me over as I turn in circles, searching for the way out. My skin prickles, and my legs and feet are wet. I start to run, challenging the mud to do its best, and sucking in air with rapid breaths as I bat away fronds of stabbing pine needles. Their electric piercing spurs me on towards the light of the meadow.

When the wood releases me in into the fresh, tingling air I stand in bewilderment gazing around me. The woods had bound me to them, entranced me and held me close. I had heard music, been lulled to sleep, and then shocked, I had run, been spat out, back to my harsh and uncaring reality. The house stands sentinel above the meadow. I trudge towards it, exhausted. I can't understand what happened, and I can't explain it, but I liked it.

Looking down at Max when I get to the house, his voice is distant, its insistence unimportant.

'Where have you been? I'm starving. Can you make me something to eat.'

It is not a question.

Chapter 5

I look at Max as he wolfs down chicken pasta, desperate to finish his meal and leave me. He is only eight years old, his birthday last week ending in dismal chaos when Conor refused to come downstairs for the cake, and I dropped it on the way upstairs to his room. Max had run into the drawing room, slamming the door and shouting, 'You care more about him than you do about me.'

Was he right? His words had been fired into my mind and had lodged there. I know that trying to help Conor is trying to help Max, but I know too, and dread, that he needs more than this from me. He needs me to help him cope with a prodigal, broken father if he is not to join Conor in his swirling sea of desolation and hopelessness.

It is harder than ever to show Max love. His cold composure rattles me when I try to engage with him, his anger frightens me when he pushes me away, and his aggressive dismissals send me into an unfeeling withdrawal. Providing emotional care is so much more taxing than cooking and cleaning. I want to understand him as a sad child who has experienced too much in his short life but the reality of dealing with rage and resentment challenges my sense of motherhood and overwhelms me. I want to try to rekindle warmth towards him but nothing I do helps him or me.

I reason with myself that he is just a sad little boy. I try to see his coldness as confusion, to understand he has no one else but me to blame, that his anger is self-protection, that he needs to push me away in case we get too close and he is abandoned again.

When the school starts reporting increased aggression from him I see an opportunity. I defend him, let myself forget that sometimes I fear for my own safety when he rampages through the house, but it is on the day that the school asks me to come in again, to explain that they were sure I understand that Max can no longer stay there, that I make the second most difficult decision of my life. I will home-school him. I will help him grow by learning with him.

It is a bad decision. In my desire to learn to love my young son I conjure up visions of the two of us spending days harnessing his love of books by poring over them together. I design days of study, nature walks, and play times for us to engage in. I will respect his need for solitude and give him time alone in the drawing room. I know that finding other children for him to play with is not possible. As long as the memories of his aggression remain alongside the ongoing certainty that this house contain a bad mother struggling to raise him alone, we will be alone together. So, we will travel to beaches and headlands where we can explore rockpools and cliff paths before consuming sandy picnics in the company of shrieking choughs and wheeling seagulls.

How wrong I was to think these dreamy days would be possible. The fighting starts from the first day. Max has always risen early. I hear him wandering the house before dawn, but when at 9.00am I tell him school-time is starting he snaps back at me that he is in the middle of something else. Every day I insist he comes to the table with worksheets, books, pens, and paper laid out on it, he refuses. I try to drag him there by force, his feet drumming on the floor as I pull his arms. If I do succeed, he sits at the table, with his face propped in one hand, mouth-downturned, eyes grey and sullen, daring me to entertain him. I thought I had done the best thing by downloading resources suitable for eight years olds from the computer in the internet café, now manned by a different but similarly disinterested teenager. I realise in the first week that I should have aimed higher to grab Max's attention.

He toys with me, first refusing to engage and then reeling off answers that he had known all along. When I offer him a choice of what to learn from the assembled pile of papers and books, he rifles through them, knocking papers onto the floor and setting pens rolling across the table, before announcing there is nothing there that he does not already know. I could add arrogance to the list of his character traits.

When he jumps down from the high-backed chair and runs off into the vastness of the house, I impose punishments by withholding reading time, confiscating his bricks, or sending him to bed. He sits them out in still silence, defying me not to feel like the punished one as I wait with fuming irritation to see any signs of remorse or apology. None ever come and I exhort myself to stay calm. I walk the gardens feeling his watchful smirk from his bedroom window behind me.

I am on edge all the time as I try to focus on this child from whom there is no respite. I feel tested to the limit, as though I am peering over the edge of a deep black abyss into which a tiny shove could plunge me. With the picture of Conor, his father, crying in the bed upstairs in my mind, I alternate between despair and anger. I live on tenterhooks, day by day awaiting the next crisis. I cannot settle and my temper shortens. I long for something other than what I have, to be absorbed in something else, to be taken away from this life. I notice too that my hair is thinning, my appetite decreasing, the horrible green pinafore dress is hanging off my skinny frame. Sleep is a longed-for but elusive retreat and I am tempted more often to reach for the Jameson at the top of the dresser in the evenings than to go to bed.

When the Context lures me out into its vast openness and offers me comfort, I take up its invitation as often as I can. The gentleness of the surroundings, the land's acceptance of me, are so contrasting to my experiences inside the house that I crave more and more of it. When I am caged inside the house I throw open the windows to let in the outside, inviting those feelings of peace to come and soothe me. When I escape, I look again for the entrancement of the woods. Sometimes I dig the earth, relishing its yielding to the grip the spade as I prepare it to accept bulbs and seeds with their promise of new life. I prune apple and pear trees, selecting boughs for shortening, watching for new fruit to nurture. When I am with them it is as though the trees and plants and grasses appreciate me, care for me. Sometimes I imagine that they whisper to me that all will be well, and my gratitude joins with their calming auras. I watch the changing seasons, and feel their challenges, celebrate their successes. All that I want to pour into Conor and Max I pour into the Context.

#

Waking early this morning I decide to take a swim in the lake, something I have not done since the terrible incident with Conor. As I wander barefoot down through the meadow my eye is caught by movement at the edge of the woods. Peering to make out what the creature is I edge closer until an emaciated pony comes into view. Her hair is matted, skin infested with sores, and hooves overgrown. I cannot understand how she has got here but as much as she is wary to approach me I have no hesitation in deciding to befriend her.

Jewel, as I came to name her, is grey, speckled with faint white spots. Her mane is darker and lies in ragged knots across her weakened neck. She stands just about my height so that her sad dark eyes are level with mine. We stand looking at each other, beseeching understanding. I reach out to touch her and she shies away with a soft whinny. I turn to walk with careful steps, clicking my tongue to encourage her to follow. I see over my shoulder that she falters as she contemplates it. Encouraged, I whisper to her that she will be safe with me. I am already thinking of the rundown stables behind the kitchen garden, knowing that with some restoration they will be a perfect home for her. When I offer her a freshly-plucked carrot she hesitates at first, but when she does take it between her velvet lips I dare to believe that she may be willing to learn to trust me.

#

With care from me Jewel recovers, and one day lets me climb onto her now strong back and walk her around the paddock. Over many months the two of us have formed a bond that gives me an outlet for my frustrations and a focus for my care. Max and Conor show no interest in her so whenever I can escape I spend time riding her, grooming her, and tending to the stable. We amble around the estate, connected to each other in silence, and feeling the air change with the seasons.

It isn't only Jewel's unquestioning acceptance of me that comforts me, it is the freedom she offers. Together we ride around the grounds, sometimes walking, sometimes galloping with a recklessness that exhilarates and scares me as it chases away my sadness and loneliness. Jewel breaks my prison walls and I feel more comfortable and at peace on her back than I do at any time inside the house. I love her in a way that I wish I could love Max.

Max's behaviour has become so difficult now that I have given up any hope of home-schooling him. His refusal to attend to me or to his books has defeated me and I have accepted that he will teach himself what he wants to learn. He locks himself away, ignoring me or rebuffing with increasing aggression my efforts to engage him. I tried to interest him in gardening so that we could do it together as Conor and I had once done, but when he pulled up the delicate shoots, pulled the heads off newly blooming flowers and stamped on the vegetables battling against the vicious wind to survive I gave up. When I found him piercing the wings of butterflies with pins and pulling the legs off beetles, I banned him from going into the garden without me.

Inside the house he finds new ways to plant seeds of horror into me. One day he presented me with a dead rabbit, saying that he had found it in the grounds. I quashed the lurch in my stomach that questioned the veracity of his statement. When I found smashed birds' eggs in his room, I asked him where he had got them from. He told me they had fallen from the nest in the tree outside his bedroom.

With some trepidation I did my best to help Max share my excitement on finding the bed that a pregnant wild cat had made at the side of our house. I explained to him that the mother was preparing a comfortable place for her babies to be born, and that I had tried to do the same for him when he was going to be born. He showed no interest, except to ask how cats died and if people ever killed them. I had to push away the thoughts his words induced, making an excuse to go up to my bedroom. He didn't mention the impending birth again and when two days later I saw four tiny screeching bundles I cooed over them on my own. The next day there was only one kitten in the bed. I never knew what happened to the other three.

I have no proof that Max is causing the deaths of these animals, but his lack of feeling fills me with dread. Far from being the nature-loving child I had fantasised about, my son is hard-hearted and seems to jinx the lives that surround him. What kind of mother am I to be capable of such appalling thoughts about my own son? I have no one to share them with and I fight the guilt and anxiety every day. I try to push the weight of them away but with each determined shove, a piece of me splinters. I am weakening, tearing into jagged pieces, alone and desperate as I face relentless rejection from the two people I am caring for.

My slow plunge into hopelessness escalated yesterday morning when I went to the stable and found it empty. The door was open, fresh straw on the floor but no sign of Jewel. My heart jumped and pounded as I began calling out for her. When she didn't come I started to search the grounds, in case she had become trapped in a bush or fence. With increasing panic I began to run, shouting for her, eyes stinging as they scanned the land. This was too much to bear. Jewel had become part of me, the only living being that understood me. She carried my fears and fantasies, and offered me concern and comfort when nothing else could. The freedom of riding her sustained me, and the thought of losing her pierced me to my core.

After hours of searching last night I left food out for her before giving in to my exhaustion, but when I rushed to her stable this morning she had not returned. My despair is complete, and I know that if I don't do something now, I will lose all remnants of my will to continue.

#

Despite his resistance, and mine, I insist on Max attending therapy. I do so with reluctance, still stinging from the fruitlessness of putting Conor through well-meaning attempts to help, and knowing that Max will hate it.

He does. By the time we arrive at the therapist's office at the hospital, a cold sterile environment despite the vase of flowers and box of tissues placed on the table underneath an abstract canvas picture, we are both red faced and burning with anger and frustration. A smiling older woman with short grey hair greets us. I shove Max through the door ahead of me, fearful that he will refuse. He trips over his feet as he stumbles into the sofa opposite her single chair.

'Hello, you must be Max,' smiles Mrs O'Donohoe, 'and you must be Max's mother.' She turns to acknowledge me. I attempt a smile, feeling the heat radiating from my face. My stomach churns at the possibility of being found out as the terrible mother I am.

'Thank you for seeing Max,' I begin. 'I can tell you a bit about him if you like.'

'I think it would better if Max tells me about himself. Why don't you wait outside? You'll find a chair and some magazines there.'

I am embarrassed to be dismissed, recognising that she does not want to hear my version of Max's problems. So, as it was with Conor, I am relegated to escort and chauffeur. I turn and leave the room to find the chair and sit on it for the fifty minutes.

Max walks straight past me when the session ends, so that I have to scoop up my bag and run to catch him up. Without a word we slide into the car, him in the back, and drive home.

After a couple of sessions Mrs O'Donohoe sends me a report: 'Max is a child who suffers from loss, which he expresses through resistance to new relationships. He has not formed a secure attachment and consequently is fearful of being left alone. He expresses this fear at times by withdrawing and detaching himself from close others, and at other times by lashing out in anger. He finds it hard to see the world through other people's eyes and so does not feel the effects of his actions on others during his periods of rage. He may well regret his behaviour later but is unable to say so.'

I can hardly read the report to the end. To me, it may as well have stated that Max has a bad mother. I have failed to provide him with security, and both he and our relationship is damaged. It may as well have said that it is all my fault that he cannot be close to anyone and so has become a sad, empty child.

She suggests tests and finds that Max is not on the autistic spectrum, he does not suffer from ADHD, there is no evidence of dyslexia. Max is a child with a vivid imagination who appears to find it hard to know that difference between the world he imagines and the world he lives in. He is of high intellect.

Max and I are given homework tasks by Mrs O'Donohoe: to spend time together, to make trips out together. Max is asked to give me compliments, to try saying thank you after meals. The suggestions, the reports, the sessions, go on forever, week after week, but I don't see any discernible difference in him or in his behaviour. His view of me and of the world is fixed, and he deals with it with anger and despair.

Chapter 6

As I walk Conor through the door of the square beige building that will be his new home, I still find it hard to believe that I have agreed to send him away. In the weeks following Jewel's disappearance, I seemed to grow new resolve to accept that I was not enough for him anymore. I don't know whether it was the sadness at the constant rejection from him and Max, or the simmering anger at suffering yet another loss, but I saw clearly for the first time, that my life could no longer be about what Conor wants and had to become about what Conor needs.

When I decided to arrange for Conor to see a psychiatrist I steeled myself to return to the GP's surgery in town, marched up to the desk and requested an appointment. This time I did not care who heard. If Conor did not change I would be the one needing professional help. I stared directly at the curious waiting patients as I left with the appointment card in my hand, daring them to say something. One by one they lowered their eyes as I strode out of the door.

I tried to explain to Conor what was going to happen, that although he was going to be living somewhere else, it was for the best and only until he got better. At first he signalled compliance with his downcast eyes but as the day for me to take him there came closer, he became angry, telling me I was sending him away, that I didn't want him anymore that this was the final straw in his dismal life.

Ever since his suicide attempt I had been living in fear of him attempting to harm himself or Max again. He assured me many times that he would not, but it was only when he was asleep that I felt brave enough to leave the house to walk the grounds.

The first thing I did in the mornings and the last thing at night was to check that he was still in the bed and not in an agitated state. At night the slightest sound would alert me, and I would rise from my bed and go to check on him again. It was like living in the shadow of a volcano that could blow at any moment and the tension rubbed my nerves raw.

When the day came for him to move to Orchard View, I didn't tell Conor where we were going. I simply helped him to dress and guided his listless body to the car, fearing with every step that he would unleash his anger. I was thankful for once that this was a day that he was inhabiting his other self and not the one that appeared to have any cognisance of what was happening.

Little expense has been spent on trying to make this building look less like an institution. Its glass doors speak of constant watchfulness, the heavy bolts of locking people in. As they are opened by a young man in a clinical white smock I am assailed by scents of bleach and air fresheners. A woman sits in a chair in the hallway picking at scabs on her face. She stares at us with mild curiosity before resuming. An old man shuffles past, head down, muttering to himself and showing us no interest. From the corridor that stretches away from the door I hear loud anguished sobbing that reminds me of Conor, and sends shivers through me.

The front office, into which we are shown, is cluttered with piles of papers and cardboard files. A whiteboard has a rota of staff on it and smiling photos of these professional carers looking out at the mess. Outside the office in an overheated foyer, pencil pictures of residents on the wall tell of attempts at working with people to recognise who they are, who they live with. The forlorn inhabitants are not loud and they don't move fast. They seem not to interact with each other. The swirls of sadness threaten to engulf me and I make one-sided banal conversation with Conor to save him and me from succumbing as the nurse who had greeted us bustles around, chattering and gathering pieces of paper for signing. I am pleased of the distraction and guide Conor through the administration, launching a flurry of questions as he fiddles with a loose thread on the cuff of his shirt.

'Will you make sure that he eats regularly? He doesn't like spicy food. He has been taking vitamin tablets, I have put some in his bag. Do you have other men the same age as him living here? Are there activities that he can take part in? He used to like being outdoors.'

The nurse is friendly and professional, introduces himself as Dave, and ignores my babbling, and instead offers reassurance.

'Don't worry, Mrs Fairman, we will take good care of him. We run a happy home here and treat all our residents with respect.'

Turning to Conor he says, 'It's alright, mate, you may find it hard to believe but you will come to enjoy life here. It won't be long before you are able to return home again.'

I try to accept the shiver of hope that feels false yet thrills through me with these last words.

Paperwork signed, Dave leads us down a corridor that winds in a square around a desolate paved courtyard planted with some brightly coloured children's windmills that fail either to turn or to cheer up the surroundings. Any view of an orchard that must have given this place its name has long been obliterated. Passing cheap prints of water and swans and rolling hills, I see doors painted institutional green. The tenth one is labelled CONOR FAIRMAN.

Pushing gently against the automatic fire regulation closing mechanism, Dave ushers us into a sparse single-bedded room containing a table that rolls over the bed and a grey stacking chair next to the single bed. I try not to show my disappointment in the room as the three of us jostle for space. Pulling out a photograph of the house I place it on the table. I had thought hard about what photo to bring, advice from the institution on the 'What to Pack' list. I knew not to provoke Conor with a photo of Max and was not confident that he wanted to be reminded even of me, so had chosen from the stack of photographs we had taken of the house when we first moved there. The image was a particularly beautiful one, showing the house in all its faded grandeur, its splendid exterior framed against a perfect blue sky with fluffy white clouds and a single bird framed within it. Keen to look busy I turn next to the small suitcase to unpack the few clothes, arranging them neatly in the single wardrobe against the far wall. With only Conor's toothbrush and a bar of soap left to place in the en-suite bathroom, I have nothing left to occupy myself with and turn back to Conor.

Dave has been taking Conor's temperature and asking him a series of questions. I heard suicide mentioned, to which, along with the many other questions Conor whispers 'No.' He is sitting on the edge of the bed, Dave standing over him, watching him take pills he has handed him in a clear plastic container that he then takes from him. He asks him for his belt and shoelaces and suggests he might like to get into his tracksuit and come and meet the other residents. I realise this is my cue to leave and am surprised by the warm surge of relief that floods my body.

'I'll leave you to it then love,' I say in an overly cheery voice, 'I'll come and see you at the weekend.'

I turn to Dave, 'Is that alright?'

Dave nods whilst extending his thumb and forefinger, holding them up to his ear and mouthing that he will call me. With a peck on Conor's shaven cheek, I stumble out of the door, feet tripping over each other in my haste to get away.

As I retrace my steps along the corridor I can see two residents walking around the desolate courtyard in its middle, one shouting and waving his hands in the air, the other walking in small circles, fingers in his ears, cowering.

When I am buzzed out of the building and am back in the carpark, there is a woman standing motionless at the fence looking out over the busy road on the other side.

'Take me home with you,' she pleads.

I almost push her aside as I reach for the car door handle and fall into the car, slamming the door shut beside me. I lean on the steering wheel and let the tears come as I fumble to get the key in the slot and rev the engine to take me and Max away from this place. Safely out on the road, I pull into the first layby we reach and, leaning on the steering wheel to cradle my head, sob until my throat is dry, my stomach is heaving and my mind is a blissful blank. Turning to Max seated in the back, I bring out my cheery voice again as I start the engine,

'Come on then, kiddo, it's just you and me again.'

Back at the house after two hours driving, the roller coaster that is relief and guilt makes me stagger across at its threshold. As I clutch at the door frame to steady myself, Max tuts and pushes past me. Taking off my coat and sitting on the hall trestle I feel a difference in the house. It does not feel like it felt when Conor disappeared, it does not feel like there is a void at its centre. It feels like it is relaxing, settling back into itself. Or is that me?

#

As Max has become adolescent he has grown taller, more menacing when he stands over me to scream his resentment into my face. His face has lost its chubby roundness and is becoming more angular, with a sharp chin speckled with wispy hairs that makes him look unkempt and dirty. The smell of his feet when he takes his trainers off is sickening and mingles with his body odour of chicken soup and sour milk. His deepening voice means that he can no longer wheedle as effectively when I deny him things, instead he roars with an intimidation that frightens me.

Max encircles himself with solitude, locking himself away in 'his' drawing room, glowering at me if I enter. My surreptitious surveys of the room show the floor scattered with used pens, large drawing pads covered with deep scored pencil drawings of houses and towns, and scribbled numerical calculations. Papers carpet the floor, dense with detail showing a frantic absorption. He stays up at nights and stays in bed during the days. Like a vampire.

With Conor away and Max keeping apart from me I have time to find myself again. I start by taking care of my body; lots of exercise, regular eating. I start to look after my hair. I trim it and use nettles from the garden to make a nourishing shampoo. I am surprised how fast my body responds to its nurture. My skin starts to take on its healthy glow of my youth, my weak muscles strengthen from hours of swimming and walking. The improvements help and I am more upright in body and mind as I go about my life.

But it's my life that is the problem. With little to distract my mind it is too easy to reminisce about all that has happened and all that I have lost. I think about Conor often. I still do not know why he left or what brought him back. He told me he had a wondrous experience but no trace of it remained in the Conor that came home, who was only lost and despairing. I am frustrated and scared in my not-knowing, but I recognise also the flames of anger kindling inside me as I yearn for an explanation. I must find something new to focus on, to quell the churn of questions and lack of answers that swirl around my head.

Today I take down Conor's photo from the dresser and place it in the drawer next to my bed, at hand but out of sight. I dig out my old sewing machine from its dusty hibernation in the loft and move it into Lacan, throwing open the shutters that have remained closed since that visit from Mr Murphy. I dust and clean, relishing the aches in my arms and legs. I drag the table from the hallway into the room and place the machine on top of it. I open the trunk in the bedroom, turning my head away against the smell of mothballs, and pull out the material Conor and I had bought together for curtains. Scarlet red with green trims. We said it represented love, for each other and for Ireland. Today it represents freedom.

Relishing the therapeutic pleasure of following one tiny stitch with another and another I start a quilt. Growing up alone in the dark empty house with Great Aunt Alice had taught me to be content with my own company. Alice had been kind and caring to the motherless child she had taken in, but by the time I came to her she was set in the ways of a woman in her seventies who had lived her adult life alone since caring for her sister until she died. Always a worker, Alice despised idleness and rose early to clean the spotless house and make the daily trip to the shops that served both her practical and social needs. She returned by 11.00 to ensure that lunch was on the table at midday, after the Angelus. Long, quiet afternoons followed, in which Alice would read and play solitaire, and, if it was a Monday or a Thursday, receive visitors. She taught me to sew on Tuesdays. Fridays and Saturdays meant going to the church to tend to the flowers and sweep the incense-dusted floors. No question that Sundays were devoted to Mass and prayer.

Alice expected me to respect her regime, fit in with it. Inviting friends to the house was never a possibility. She hated noise and disruption and it gave her a headache, so I learnt to be resourceful in entertaining myself. Making quilts became a solace for me, the tiny stitches around neat squares requiring therapeutic concentration that shut out anything else.

My first quilt sewn as an adult is splendid. Its shimmering, noble red, offset with trims of green reminds me of how my anger can be quelled by nature. It is the perfect size for the double bed that had been mine and Conor's, and I allocated fifty squares to my side and fifty to his in the hope that one day we will share it again.

I love the peace that my sewing brings now that Max leaves me undisturbed for hours. For material I move onto Max's baby clothes and blankets. Each quilt represents my past and new beginnings as the squares of clothes lock into fresh embraces with each other. I contemplate using Conor's clothes but when I pick up a shirt of his, tailor scissors in hand, I am thrown back to the past by the faint smell of Conor mingling with musty odours and I can't do it. I tell myself that he will need his clothes when he comes back home, and place them back in the wardrobe.

Most days I can get outside to the garden too. I tend to my vegetable plots and turn the land around Jewel's now collapsed stable into a mini arboretum. I select each tree for its hardiness and plant it for people who have been in my life. Doing things with my hands again has become so effective in bringing me calm that I long for new things to keep them busy. I teach myself jewellery-making, knitting, I paint. I am using this proliferation of activities to lose myself, and they serve me well in removing me from the reality of my lonely life.

I fall into a pattern of waking up early, swimming, making breakfast for Max and leaving it in the Aga for him, often finding it still there in the evening. I remove myself to work in Lacan, giving myself a small kiss of pride with each item created. When I hear Max moving around the house, from his drawing-room to the bathroom, sometimes into the kitchen for a snack, and then, to my relief back to his drawing-room, I get distracted. I hold my breath, listen, head cocked, waiting with anxiety kicking at my stomach. I don't want him to come into my room, my studio, demanding, shouting, whining. I want to preserve my peace, my escape. The click of the drawing room door closing is my cue to breathe again, to taste the silence. I let out my breath and bend my head back over my task.

I am struggling on with trying to meet Max's emotional needs but no matter what I do I cannot meet his growing material demands. He craves the trainers, football team jumpers that he sees on other teenagers. He wants an endless supply of books, paper, pens. I am pleased that he wants to be like others of his age, and I want to support him, but I don't have the money to supply him with what he wants.

I have always managed financially by juggling government benefits with support I can provide myself – the food grown on our land, the eggs and bodies of the chickens, clothes made by me although they are now eschewed with a sneer by Max. I have taken to leaving the vegetables and eggs that we don't eat by the main gate for passers-by, with a box for donations, the sparse coins providing a thin income for us. We live sparsely but I pride myself on finding ways to minimise reliance on others.

It is Max though who points out to me one day that I have "mountains of this crap you make. Eejits would pay good money for this." He is right. I have made so many quilts, boxes of jewellery, and hand-embroidered table napkins that I have had to use a spare bedroom to store them in. With his harsh words, Max has provided the key to my new life.

#

On my first day at the weekly Country Market, held in the town square I make 100 Euros in the first three hours. My shamrock pendants (20 euro each) are popular, as are my beaten silver bangles (5 euro each or three for 12 euro). I am delighted. I feel the thrill of anticipation as I stand in my battered anorak, hood up when it is raining, and pulled off my face as soon as it stops, to watch tourists and locals approach the stall with curiosity. The excitement of filling my wallet is new, being alone and in charge of my own destiny is thrilling.

'You look happy,' are Rosie's first words to me. 'Had a good morning?'

I stare at the heavy middle-aged woman wearing a flowing flowery dress over a pair of black wellington boots, smiling at me with an awkward turn of her head as she packs the van behind the neighbouring stall with large bags of dog food, feeding bowls for cats, bedding for hamsters and guinea pigs, and various other pet accessories. She chatters on, panting for breath as she heaves her goods:

'I never know what sort of trade I am going to get. Very few people round here have pets but the ones that do are happy to spend the money on them. Ooh come here, I laughed last week, I had a tourist asking if I sold body warmers for cats. Ha! I mean honestly. Can you imagine the farm cats round here being given a body warmer?'

She gave an infectious loud laugh, and I couldn't resist a nervous smile.

'Aah look at him, you alright Jimmy?' she calls across the car park lined with market stalls to the man with a brown wrinkled face shuffling off with an empty carrier bag billowing in his hand,

'He comes every week to sell carrots and parsnips from his farm. Doesn't speak to anyone, just sits on a chair waiting for his six bunches of veg to sell and then goes to the pub with the proceeds. Good on him. Poor Jimmy lost his wife years ago. Says that the fairies took her to nurse one of their babies.'

She rolled her eyes and tapped the side of her head with one finger, 'Anyway that's me done. See you next week.'

The rattle of her car and the exhaust fumes it blew over me did nothing to quell my pleasure as I turned back to my goods and surveyed them with pride. I am a market trader! The fumes are soon camouflaged by the odours of chicken manure, horse droppings, fresh bread, and coffee of the busy market and to me they smell of adventure.

I don't want this morning to end. The bustle of the market as stallholders pack away, the lingering tourists sipping coffee watching the activity, the occasional crow of a caged rooster who will not be sold today, all plant new life in me. This everyday world is one I want to join. I wander over to a coffee stall, wanting and not wanting some more human company.

'You're lucky girleen, I am just about to pack up. Haven't see you around here before,' says the middle-aged, bearded, rather handsome barista, as he shouts over the machine's hisses and steams.

'I'm new. I sell the quilts and jewellery on the stall over there,' I point at my empty table.

'Welcome then. This one's on me. I hope it's the first of many more,' he hands me the steaming cup and winks.

I am surprised that I smile back at him from under cast-down eyes.

#

I love my Saturdays at the market. I have extended my range of goods to include painted flowerpots that I find around my land. I am thrilled to be commissioned to make a personalised house name plate, *Gallan Cottage*, by one of the second-home owners who frequent the area. My weeks are full now, working away to ensure I have a good selection to take with me on Saturdays. Now, after only six Saturdays, mine is a stall that regular customers seek out.

'I've got my niece's wedding coming up. She'd love a set of your table napkins.'

'My daughter has just moved to a new house. Would you ever be able to make an Irish linen tablecloth for her?'

'Help. It's my dad's birthday tomorrow- have you anything I can get for him?'

Of course, part of my exhilaration is the extra money that I now have. It's not a fortune but it's a way of buying some of the things that Max wants. It isn't that he is grateful, more that it keeps him quiet, leaves me alone. He used to whine when I prepared to set off on Saturday mornings. He doesn't want me at home but he hates to see me doing things that I am happy with, without him.

At first he tried to sabotage my new outings. He pretended he was ill, refused to eat, said he wanted to talk to me and then would sit in stony silence. Sometimes he just shouted at me and called me selfish for doing my own thing and leaving him home alone.

His behaviour changed when he came to understand the link between me going to the market and him getting the material goods that he wanted. He never helps me load the car, and never comes with me to the market but now he makes a point of telling me that he is happy for me to go and that he hopes I make a lot of money this week. He usually follows this by telling me the latest item that he wants. I listen in silence before I head off to my few hours in a world of satisfaction and fulfilment.

Rosie remains as friendly as she had been at our first meeting, always chattering and laughing, never seeming to need an answer from me but welcoming one if she gets it. I learn that she lives in the town with two teenage daughters who always seemed to be in one scrape or another.

'My Maria, you'll never guess, she's only gone and got her tractor's licence. Clear the roads!' she shrieks with laughter and beams with pride. 'Of course, she's been helping out on the farm ever since her father died, so she's been driving the tractor for years, but she never told me she was applying to make it legal. She's a good girl. Don't know what I'd without her.'

The words sound strange in my ears. Here is another mother bringing up a child without a father, and enjoying it. She doesn't tell me why she is alone in her parenting, and I don't ask, but her cheery and positive approach to it is exhilarating. Rosie makes no efforts to hide how much she loves her daughters, likes having them around. There are new stories every week of their achievements, stories they have told her, things they have done for her, as well as mischief they have got up to. The contrast with my own mothering experience taps at the pit of my stomach as Rosie describes the relationships with her children. They are picture book ideals to me. She is the mother I had dreamed of being when I was a child. I am envious and intrigued. I want to get closer to Rosie, see her mothering for myself, and perhaps, maybe, who knows, even learn how to achieve the same with Max.

Rosie and I fall into a pattern of starting our mornings at the market with a cup of coffee, bought from the man with whom I now have a tentative flirtatious banter with. Whoever arrives first buys the coffees. This is the nearest to a friendship that I have had in the ten years I have lived here. I love being included, of having notice taken of me, of having someone to expect me. It's been so long since anyone has done anything for me, that at first I am scared and unsure of how to reciprocate. Rosie is so open about her life, and never asks about mine. She must know who I am, where I live, who I live with, but she is undemanding, wanting only a listener. I am happy to oblige.

Rosie's outgoing personality and long-standing as a market-stall holder means that all the other stallholders know and like her. Her stall is the hub for gatherings for gossip and chat. At first I stand back only listening, wanting to join in but intimidated by the fast-paced chatter. The talk is light, dosed with humour, tales of annoying husbands, errant children, provocative weather. I love hearing the stories of everyday life of other people. My own has been so different and I am relieved that there is no expectation for me to share it. They must know my situation, absent husband and 'difficult' child, but there seems to be an unspoken agreement not to press me for details.

Rosie, always made the effort to introduce me, saying with a casual wave in my direction, 'This is Marianne, from the big house', her eyes catching theirs' to share the unspoken knowledge of which the 'big house' is. 'Marianne, this is Anne-Marie, Peg, Aoise, Sean…'

I had not told Rosie where I lived so the first time she said it I recoiled, alarmed about what they knew, fearful that once people made the connection I would be ostracised. Some of them would be parents of children who had been victims of Max's bullying. Others would have heard about my husband disappearing when I was pregnant, returning as a broken man and now committed to a psychiatric institution, but nothing was said until …

'So weird what happened to you. Do you ever think it was the fairies took him?'

I stared at the speaker, a woman named Cathleen. How I longed to believe that his disappearance could be explained, but this possibility seemed as fantastical as the talk of the other world that Conor said he had seen for one night.

'The fairies? What on earth do you mean?' I gasped.

'Oh, you know don't you that your house was built on fairy land? Blocks their path to battle. It has always had misfortune, you know. Why do you think it was empty for so long? Maybe they led him away in revenge? Took him away to their world.'

Rosie butted in, 'Oh for goodness sake Cathleen, leave the poor woman alone. she's had enough to deal with without your ridiculous suggestions.'

Rosie managed to be both assertive and friendly in killing this conversation, but it stayed in my head for a long time afterwards.

#

Today is freezing. A sheet of grey sky sits low over the dark January morning. I am woken by wind whistling down the chimney, trickling soot into the unused grate. The room is extra dark and pulling back the curtain does nothing to rouse my reluctance to be out of bed. The hills I gaze at are hidden in a mist that halves their height, and bare branches of the trees in the woods fight against the wind.

It is no better when I reach the market and start to wrestle with my marquee. I combat the wind's attempts at smothering my neon pink tablecloth and lay out my selection of earrings and bangles with some fear they will be whipped away by a triumphant gust. The smell of wet faux fur begins to irritate me as I hug myself into my anorak and hunch down into my chair waiting for Rosie, and custom.

By midday I have sold one pair of earrings: 11 Euros. The market is desolate, bereft even of the small regular crowd of locals. Only the whipping of canvas and the occasional bang of a board being blown to the ground can be heard, the roosters and the chicks silenced as they huddle into the corners of their dismal prisons. Soggy cake wrappings blow through the air. The smell today is of wetness, clinging and chilling. The few customers who clomp past my stall, heads down, are in no mood to peruse jewellery, wanting only to escape the sting of the rain. Even Rosie is quiet today, giving up on calling across to me against the wind's howl, and instead sliding down her chair, arms wrapped around herself. The warmth of our coffee is futile against dropping temperatures and moods today.

'If I haven't got a cold coming on I'll eat Jimmy's flat cap,' Rosie says as she nods across the tarmac.

Jimmy is sitting as usual, proud and upright on his folding chair, oblivious to the rain dripping from his brown tweed cap onto his nose and down his chin. At his feet laid out on a on a plastic carrier bag are bunches of beetroot and carrots, and some potatoes. He nods back at us.

'The fairies are at work today,' he mutters

When the thunder cracks so does Rosie.

'Right that's it, I'm off. Sod this,' she says and starts to pack up.

It is enough for me to concede defeat too. With the jewellery stowed alongside me on the passenger seat I drive home feeling like a naughty schoolgirl skipping class. As I turn into the gates the usual dread descends on me. I know Max will be glowering and waiting for me when I reach the house, eager to find out how much money I have made. He is fourteen now, no longer making any pretence to be other than a man sharing a house with me. I am not his mother, only a maid, and chef. Our interactions are short and curt and we each pursue our own lives within and outside the house that accepts our separateness with a heavy silence.

At the end of the drive I sit looking at this house, the place that once held so many possibilities and now offers only space. I am soothed by the rhythmic swishing of the windscreen wipers, sharing the futility of their fight against the rain. Reluctant to step into it for another drenching I let myself drift into my favourite daydream.

I will enter the house and be greeted with a cheery hello from Max as he comes to welcome me home with a hot chocolate. He will urge me to come and sit in the drawing room where he has coaxed a fire to life using sticks he has gathered from our woods. As I sit there with my son, sipping my chocolate he will ask me about my morning, sympathising with its challenges and reassuring me that it doesn't matter, all will be better next weekend. As I drift into a snooze he will carefully take the cup, lay a blanket over me, and creep out of the room, leaving the door open in case I wake and need anything.

Daydream over, I sigh and make the dash for the front door. Inside, I squeeze out of my wellington boots, pull off my sodden socks, and shake the water off my anorak. Once freed of its clinging dampness I wipe my hands on my smock, planning lunch in my head. The deafening silence of the house coddles me as I plod downstairs to the kitchen, where I soak up its warmth whilst boiling an egg.

Chapter 7

Shoulders back, head up and smiling, I always knock as I enter Conor's room. Over the years the medication's effects have become less so dramatic. He slurs his words less often and his eyes have settled into a dreamy squint rather than being half-closed. Propped upright in bed with four pillows in crisp white cotton, and wearing the pyjamas I had brought up for him on my previous visit, red stripes on a pale blue background, he doesn't acknowledge my entry into his room. His pale, thin face stares straight ahead, and his hands sit above the covers, fidgeting with each other.

'Hello darling, how are you feeling?' I say, 'Have you seen the beautiful weather outside, it feels like the South of France out there.'

Nothing.

'We can go out into the garden if you want to? Take a little stroll? Go and visit the rabbits? If you are tired we can just sit in the sun for five minutes?' Anything, something, I think.

Nothing.

I am so tired of communicating with Conor in questions. He rarely answers and they became more pointless with every visit. I smile through and babble on with unanswered queries. If only he would say something, do something, acknowledge me, even shout at me, anything other than this silence.

The truth is that as time has gone on the questions serve a different purpose for me. They are less out of concern now, more to mask my weakening resilience. I am tired of trying and tired of being unrewarded. I get nothing out of the relationship anymore and nothing I say or do makes any difference. I may as well not be here. The weekly visits have become more demanding, less fulfilling over the years and I began to reduce them to fortnightly, monthly and now three-monthly excursions. The need to reach deeper and deeper inside myself to find the strength and some desire to make the trip becomes harder each time.

When Conor first moved to Orchard View, Max and I made the two-hour trip every Sunday, only for him to remain in the car when we arrived. I spent more time with the staff in those days than I did with Conor. I have had so many discussions with them over the years, wondering about his medication, what physical therapies he is doing, suggesting they take him down to the local shops, to the cinema. I asked whether he participated in the organised activities, the sing-songs, the visits from animals with their owners, the slideshows of other people's adventures. The staff were, and still are, always pleasant and willing to talk with me, reassuring me that everything they can do is being done for him, that Conor is watched all the time to make sure he makes no attempt to go to the 'other world' that he talks about still, but when they tell me to try and stay positive my heart drops, and I ask myself 'why?'

After seven years he remains flat and emotionless, occasionally muttering the words of the Yeats poem under his breath, looking guiltily around as he recalls the therapist's attempts to help him stop fixating on it. I make inane talk about him looking better, appearing brighter, tell him we are missing him at home. The idea of him returning to us has been sucked into the same black hole that has sucked in the man that once was Conor. His listless despair has taken possession of him so that his only interest is in his own melancholia.

#

When I draw up to Conor's home today there is nothing to indicate the horror of what I am about to experience.

Tripping up the path, I am taken by surprise when the large front door swings open and the manager stumbles out

'Oh Mrs Fairman,' she says, with a falter.

'Hello, Jane. How has Conor been?'

I cannot read her face. I am used to being given upbeat descriptions of a downbeat Conor when I visit. This is something new. Jane is speechless, rummaging through her vocabulary to find words. Something has happened, something that words cannot express. My heart drops into the swirling pit of my stomach and I know.

I stare at the manager's eyes, with my own wide and imploring. She doesn't want to say it, I don't want to hear it. I search her face, wanting but not wanting her to speak. I start to move to push past her into the house.

'I'll go up and see Conor,' I say.

'You can't. Stop. Don't. He's not there, he's gone. He's dead.' she stutters.

I stare at her as the world grinds to a halt. Stillness saturates the surroundings and I see Jane in slow motion reaching out for me as I start to fall. She guides me inside to the glass-fronted office, asking one of the nurses to bring me a cup of sweet tea. Her words wash over me in waves, coming and going in segments that spin into my head; ''unexpected', 'peaceful', can't explain it', 'no sign he was going to do it.'

My brain struggles to make sense of this. All the staff are at a loss to explain how Conor died. He had simply slipped away in his sleep last night with no cause for any concern during the previous day. With my hands clutched together between my knees to control my shaking all I can think is that this wasn't supposed to happen, Conor was supposed to be safe here, that this can't be how our dream ends. Whilst he was alive I could hold onto the possibility of him returning home. Now that he isn't, there is nothing more to hope for.

The aura of shock around the nurses mingles with flickers of their guilt as they fidget around me with white faces and furrowed foreheads. They want to comfort me, but they may as well be talking about a trip to the moon. They are trying to explain that he slipped away in the night, that they found him dead in the morning, that there was no reason to have expected it. The agony of my numbness is something I will miss when the reality starts to hit in sharp stabs over the next few days. For now though, I sit and smile at them, saying nothing. I had come to know some of them over the years and can sense their upset. I don't want to add to it with blame. Deep inside me I know that Conor has pined away, succumbing to his longing for the world he discovered and could never find the way back to.

Jane is reluctant to let me leave, questioning my ability to drive, knowing I will be alone, but after three hours I am insistent that I need to be back in the house where Conor and I had lived. I want to be close to the Conor I had loved and to be away from this place that reminds me of what he became. I need the drive to help me push away the creeping guilt about his death. And besides, I have to go back to tell Max his father has died.

As I draw up to the house it looks sort of sagged into itself, defeated. When I enter it screams Conor's absence in a new finality. I call for Max but get no reply. His jacket is missing from the hook behind the front door. A relief but I don't know what to do with myself now that I am here. I wander around, looking in on rooms on the ground floor, I make myself a cup of tea that I don't drink. I rue that it is too dark to look for eggs in the henhouse. I shuffle the pile of bills and junk mail on the kitchen dresser. I am exhausted but it feels wrong to go to bed as though nothing has happened. Besides, I am scared to try to sleep. I start to run a bath and pour myself a Jameson. I remember about the bath when I hear the water start to overflow.

I gaze at the slightly freckled, tanned face of the young newly-wed Conor in the photo I have taken from my bedside drawer. Through tears I scan his face for signs of what was to come and see only happiness. I long to be back in those days when we had just moved into the house.

'Oh you and your boarding school ways,' I laugh. Conor is folding tee-shirts into neat squares to squeeze into the bottom two drawers of the tallboy. 'You're not at school now. We have all the space we need. You don't have to fit everything into one chest of drawers.'

'Ha, you're a fine one to talk,' he retorts. 'What would the saintly Great Aunt Alice make of her ward's messy ways? I bet she wouldn't have put up with knickers on the floor and shoes strewn everywhere.'

'That's not fair, Con.' Still laughing, I pick up two black pump shoes 'See these? These are one of the only two pairs of shoes that I own. The other is a pair of wellington boots. As for my knickers, I think we both know why they are on the floor huh? Isn't it more a question of what Aunt Alice would have made of the randy old goat that I married?'

He kisses me on the cheek and wraps his arms around me as we gaze out of the window at the dark, grumbling sky, so low that it seems to tent the lawn. Through the gleam of the window, newly cleaned with vinegar and old newspaper, we can make out the shadows of ghostly trees in the woods, housing wood pigeons, magpies, maybe an owl or two, seeking shelter from the impending storm. We know that each other is suppressing a sigh of relief that our decision to go to bed instead of working on the kitchen garden can be justified by the weather chaos that is about to arrive. The prickle of our just-dry skin from our lake swim adds to our sense of wellbeing.

'You are going to have to move that chicken coop, Conor,' I say. 'I won't be able to sleep with that smell wafting up through the window.'

'Well aren't you the romantic one,' he says, eyes crinkling as he laughs at me.

We decide that today is a kitchen day, that Conor will fix the broken washing machine and I will clean up the Aga, clogged with generations of grease and oil. I joke to Conor that after this job I will need to climb into the washing machine when it is fixed.

We work together with the radio playing for a couple of hours.

'Ugh, I can't stand this anymore, Conor,' I say, black, oily hands held as far away from me as possible. 'I'm stopping for today. Let me know when you get the machine fixed.'

Conor grunts up at me from where he is lying on the floor, reaching underneath the washing machine, and winks. I go upstairs to scrub my hands.

'That's that then love. All done. I'm off for a pint,' Conor calls up the stairs. 'Have fun doing the laundry.'

He ducks as I fire a pair of boxer shorts down the stairwell at his head. 'Don't be too late,' I laugh. 'And don't forget to take a torch.'

'And you don't forget how much I love you,' comes the reply.

When I hear the crash of the front door closing I rush to rummage in the top drawer amongst my underwear. Pulling out the pregnancy test kit buried there I cross the landing to the bathroom, and close and lock the door.

The rattle of a loose window in a gust of window jolts me out of my reverie. I shuffle downstairs to the kitchen and in an automatic movement put the kettle on the Aga hotplate, but then change my mind and reach to the top of the dresser for the bottle of Jameson.

#

Time contorts like an acid trip in the days running up to Conor's funeral. The better days whistle past in a flurry of administration and funeral arrangements. The others are slow and empty as I roam the house and garden looking for distraction from torturing voices, 'He's gone, he's never coming back.' I argue back by scrubbing and mopping and steam cleaning every surface of the house. When I finish inside I move outside to power wash the walls, creating a contrast of gleaming white with dirty grey between the height I could reach and the expanses of wall above. The car gleams more brightly than it has ever done since leaving the forecourt of the dealership, and there is not a single stray leaf on the gravel of the driveway.

As Conor had died unattended, an autopsy is necessary. In the limbo of waiting for its results there is one word that clatters around my head: 'Suicide'. The staff at Orchard View have no explanation, but I do - he pined away. The challenges of having to remain in this world rather than return to one he so longed to return to were too much for him. Despair overcame him until the yearning broke his will to live. This to me explained everything. Even when the coroner returned the verdict of natural causes.

When I heard Max emerging from his room the day after I returned from Orchard View on that dreadful day I called out to him, ignoring the thumping dread in my stomach.

'Max, can you come in here please.'

I heard his loud sigh even before he had descended the stairs to the basement kitchen. When he thrust open the door, hair standing on end from lying in bed, wearing boxer shorts and a stained tee-shirt, and threw himself into a chair with a scowl, I knew that this was not going to be made easy for me.

'Can I have some…' he started

'Max, I have something to tell you.'

'Ok but can I have some bacon first?'

'No, Max, I have to tell you something first. It's important.'

'What is it that's so important then?'

I felt the urge to shake him but suppressed it.

'Max, Conor has died. He slipped away in his sleep the night before last. It was a surprise to the staff and there was nothing to be done when they found him in the morning.'

Max said nothing as the storm brewed. When it came, it blasted from him with a fury that bounced off the hard surfaces surrounding us in the kitchen.

'What a bunch of incompetent idiots. What the bloody hell were they doing? Why was no one watching him? Did no one see the signs? It's not as if he hasn't tried something like this before.'

He cursed the staff, the residents, the building, the healthcare system, without drawing breath, and I knew who would be next in the firing line.

'And what about you? Did you not notice anything last time you were up? Did he not say anything? Did you think to check his state of mind? Perhaps if you had visited more often…'

On and on he went, expertly pressing every button labelled 'guilt' within me but I let him rage, watching his face, trying not to listen to his words. As I did, I saw desperate sadness. Guilt, grief, loss overwhelmed this overgrown, selfish man-child, and came out as anger. He knew no other way of dealing with these sharp emotions. Perhaps he, like me, had believed that one day his father would return and now being told that it will never happen, the hurt was pouring out of him in this tirade.

Neither of us cried. He held back his tears with anger, I held mine back with determination not to be cowed. When his outburst stopped, he panted and glared at me, from eyes that smouldered like coals, before making his final thrust.

'You know what? I'll get something to eat in town,' he spat, his chair screeching against the floor before falling over as he hurled himself out of it.

I was surprised to find myself panting too in the intensity of the emptiness he left behind. Only when my breathing became regular again and my heart stopped thumping did I feel my sadness that my son had not asked me how I was feeling.

#

Over the past two weeks Max has made no more mention of that evening or of Conor's death, except to state that he will not be doing a reading at the service. My fear now is whether he will even attend it. The limp Orders of Service, with the picture of Conor smiling and suntanned on the front, make a forlorn, thin pile on the kitchen table. My hands tremble as I read through one of them. I don't expect many people from the town to come and it had caused me a disproportionate amount of anxiety to decide how many to order.

'Order twenty-five and be done with it' were Rosie's wise words. 'If any more mourners than that turn up then they will just have to share.'

To my surprise, a group of the pub regulars called to the house yesterday. Rosie was the only person who ever called the house. The other market stall-holders were my 'Saturday friends', with whom I chatted in superficial relaxed ways but I rarely saw them otherwise. The gossip and judgement of me and of Max still rang around the town so I had continued to avoid people whenever I could. So, to see four men ambling up the drive, caps in hand and muttering to each other as they looked at the house and gardens was an unusual sight. I was sitting in my favourite armchair with a book I could not concentrate on when I spotted them. I squinted from behind the safety of the window to make out if I recognised any. One was the barista from the market and that reassured me.

There was no preamble when I opened the front door to them.

'We'll dig the grave for ye,' one of them muttered, shuffling where he stood.

I was confused. I didn't know that it was a tradition for friends and neighbours to prepare a grave for neighbours who had died. Trying to explain to these well-meaning men that I had organised a cremation was hard, and turning them away without a job to do felt like a rejection. I ran after them as they paraded back down the driveway.

'Perhaps a reception could be held in the pub?' I stuttered.

'Grand so,' came the response, followed by, 'and when will the wake be?'

I shuddered. The idea of Conor's body being laid out in the house, and the house invaded by strangers coming to pay respects was petrifying. I could only say 'I'm not having one' before turning and running back into the house. I knew that my behaviour around the death rituals would provide yet more source of gossip.

My other unusual visitor had been the celebrant. I had known to expect her after calling her from Rosie's house but was still surprised when a smiling woman who looked no more than thirty years old, dressed in a houndstooth jacket and black trousers matching her wavy black hair approached the front door.

'Hello, I'm Margaret and I will be leading the ceremony on Thursday. Can I come in for a chat about it. You can tell me a little about how you would like to remember Conor.'

Blood rushed through me so that I swayed a little on the doorstep. I know exactly how I would like to remember Conor but that would mean obliterating the last nine years. I don't know how I can explain that to this stranger.

'I like to think that these services are not just about the person we have lost but also about those who have been left. He is at peace now but it is us who are suffering with the loss of him,' she continued.

Her acknowledgement of me as suffering prompted the threat of tears but I fought to stop them falling. I had not cried for Conor yet and I did not want the first fall to be for myself. Stiffening myself I said, 'If you mean that, I would like him to be remembered as a man who sought happiness by bringing it to others. As a man who strove to create a world of love and acceptance. As a husband whose gentleness and understanding meant it was easy to love him.'

Margaret smiled at me as she said, 'He sounds like someone who made a mark. People like that are never forgotten.'

'He changed my life,' I whispered.

The tears are so close now. If only she knew in how many ways he changed my life, the love, and the loss he has left me with. To tell her though would risk opening the gates to the flood of grief that I am holding back for fear of never recovering from the deluge that will follow.

'I would like people to know that he was a man whose only thoughts were to care for others. The man who has died was not that man. I would like people to know that he was loved to the end and did not deserve what happened to him.'

I dread that she will ask me what did happen to him, ask me to explain the unexplainable. Worse, that she will ask what is happening to me. She did not and we talked some more about readings and music for the cremation, and feeling like a fraud I managed not to tell her about his rejection of his son and wife, nor of his belief that a better world than this one existed that was forbidden to him, and killed him. Margaret did her best to be supportive, gave platitudes about the mysteries of life, and although they were meaningless to me I smiled back her as I batted them away.

After twenty minutes Margaret left, smiling with sadness in her eyes as though I was the one who was dying.

#

The rain today feels inevitable, like my inability to cry. It's insistent drumming on the windows of the house as I get ready beats in sync with my heart. Today is not just about the death of Conor, it is about the death of my hopes; my hopes for a family, to be a loving mother and wife supported by a loving husband. The flames will consume them as they will Conor.

I had worried about what to wear for days. The shapeless green pinafore had been discarded some months ago but I had few clothes to replace it, and none suitable for a funeral service. I tend to dress in jeans and a jumper most days now, trainers or wellington boots on my feet. I had wondered about making something new but could not decide on colour, style, shape nor settle down to put needle to cloth. The strangeness of preparing for my husband's cremation has rendered my hands with a mind of their own, and I use them to clean instead, searching the house for an untouched shelf or cupboard. By scrubbing away household dirt I can try to scrub away my dreams and pretend none of this is happening.

It is Rosie, of course, who appears one day with five dresses of her own for me to choose from. We laughed when I put on the first one, flowing on her large frame, voluminous on mine. The fourth one was an emerald green, straight to the knee and woollen, hidden away by Rosie 'until she lost the weight again.' Teaming it with a red scarf, I knew this was the one. They were the colours of our love.

'You look perfect, Marianne, elegant and sombre. I would be honoured if you would wear it,' she had said.

Donning the dress now, and scratching on some eyeliner and mascara, and a slick of dried up lipstick, I look at myself in the mirror. A stranger, with blackened eyes doing nothing to disguise her weariness looks back at me. I spoke to her.

'Today you close one chapter and open a new one, my girl. You can do it. You have to do it for Conor, for Max, and for yourself.'

I had never missed not having a telephone in the house until now. Registry office, funeral parlour, doctor's surgery, all needed contacting, and that was the perfect excuse to spend time at Rosie's.

Rosie understands me. She does not probe but is always ready to listen. Our bond is like a silken bungee cord. She can read me and draw me closer when I want it, and release me gently back into my own space when I am ready. I had long ago told her the full story of my marriage, and with hugs and chats and cups of tea she listened as I navigated my confusion. How I loved Conor and hated him too. How I missed him but didn't want the broken Conor back. She never offers platitudes nor judgement, sensing the whirlwind that had whistled around my heart during the years that Conor was at Orchard View. She always knew when to help me calm my anger and when to let it rage. Her house had become a safe and embracing haven for me, with Rosie at its calming centre. Now I needed her more than ever.

With a final brush of my hair, trimmed with kitchen scissors the night before, I walk the short distance to the chapel that serves many more funerals than cremations. Pushing open its heavy door I am assailed with a curious mixture of incense and mustiness. I had expected the incense smell, but the mustiness surprises me. Surely people die regularly enough to air the building?

The heels of my shoes pacing towards the front pew match the beat of the rain, and send echoing drumbeats around the small room. My heart is still, hardly even beating. I feel nothing. When I reach the front pew I don't know what to do.

Standing, I look at the small bouquets of flowers, framing the space at the front that will be occupied soon with Conor's coffin. I wish that I had thought to bring flowers from the garden. Why didn't I think of it? I was so wrapped up in myself that I hadn't thought of what Conor might want. Maybe I have time to run home and gather some? As I am contemplating this nonsensical idea, I hear the groan of the door and turn to see Max striding towards me.

He has made an effort to look smart. His sandy hair is brushed, in need of a cut but tamer than usual, and clean. He has on a pair of black chinos that he wears for his nights out, and a white shirt that he must have ironed himself. A navy-blue blazer with gold buttons makes him look like a man twice his age. I am flooded with gratitude that he has come.

'Do I have to sit at the front?' are his first words to me.

'No but I would like you to.'

The flatness of my voice conveys that I am not going to argue with him today.

He steps into the pew sideways and sits with a soft thump on the hard, narrow bench, two people's worth of space between us.

Before we can consider what to say to each other, Margaret appears through a door at the front, smiling.

'Marianne, welcome. And you must be Max?' she stretches her hand to him and he gives it a brief shake without standing up.

'Sorry, Margaret, he's…' I begin to apologise

'Not at all, Marianne, today is for you and Max. We all grieve in different ways.'

Goodness knows what she makes of this surly son who I had made so little mention of in our meeting two days before.

'Shall we go outside? The coffin is about to arrive.'

I have to nudge Max to move along the pew and out into the aisle and the two of us follow Margaret to the front door. When she opens it and we step out into the covered entry I stop in surprise. There must be fifty people there, waiting in silent mummering. They look up at me when I step out and it is with relief that I spot Rosie pushing through them. I recognise the market traders and some of the men who came to the house but the others are strangers to me. Several bow their heads as the hearse draws up but a few step forward to receive it. It takes me a minute to realise that this are not the funeral parlour pallbearers but the men from the pub. As they arrange it on their shoulders a couple gesture to Max to take the space at the front. He shakes his head and lowers his eyes, his hair flopping forward. Turning back to their task the men make a final adjustment and start the slow walk to the front platform. As I fall in behind them I feel a gentle squeeze on my hand and I am grateful to Rosie for helping me forget that Max is not at my side.

He does stand with me in the front pew. His back is stiff, eyes locked on something invisible just to the left of the coffin. I think his eyes are gleaming but he shrugs away my tentative arm as I reach to pat his shoulder. I notice that he stands only one person apart from me until the ceremony is over.

As the coffin rolls through the curtains into the roar of fire I feel a tightening around my heart. It is hard to breathe. Nothing moves except the coffin. I am rigid, shoulders hunched, insides hardened. My mind is silent, and my eyes fixed on the last physical remnants of my dream with Conor, until the electric whirr of the curtains brings faded red velvet across the gap. Still staring at them I sense movement at my side. Max is leaving, edging sideways along the pew and out into the aisle. His footsteps are the only sound as he strides towards the door, the congregation remaining where they are, watching him, assuming grief is driving his actions.

As the door of the chapel clunks shut behind him I see Margaret beckon me towards where she is standing by a door behind the furnace. I imitate the sideways shuffle that Max had performed only a minute before to exit the pew and walk towards her, head bent, breathing even and slow.

I wait with her as in ones and twos, the friends and the curious, shake my hand muttering sympathies with words I don't hear. I return their handshakes, give a half-smile and struggle to remain upright.

At last, I see Rosie approaching in the queue. She is behind a very old man who is clutching a shabby brown tweed flat cap, and a neat tidy woman with tight grey curls. She introduces herself as the owner of the pub and tells me she remembers how much she had liked Conor. She does not mention the night he disappeared but I feel the heavy breath of the elephant as she murmurs condolences. And then, wonderfully, I feel an arm around my shoulder and see Rosie, eyes wet and glistening, body strong enough to hold me as I lean into her to complete my task of accepting condolences from people I don't know.

When the queue ends, I let her guide me into the sunshine of the memorial garden where we join people standing about, unsure of what to say or do. I notice a small collection of bouquets and wonder who has brought them. I lean over to read the cards.

'With thanks for all you did for us.'

'You are missed'

'Safe in God's hands now.'

Most were signed with names I do not know. It is as if I am reading the wrong cards but it seems that Conor has touched many people in his short time amongst them. Even with the intervening years, he has been remembered and it becomes easier to replace confusion with gratitude as we stand in the sunshine. They were not there for me but, for Conor, who touched their hearts as well as mine. It is a comfort.

When the small groups of people begin to walk away, some with surreptitious looks at me, Rosie says, 'Are you ready to go to the reception, love?'

My stomach drops. The idea of the reception scares me. Am I the bereaved wife to these people or still the wanton woman? The errant mother?

'Do we have to Rosie?'

'I think it's important, sweetheart. It may help you. Let's go and we can leave as soon as you are ready.'

I have no strength to resist, so in my daze of grief, I allow Rosie to lead me to her battered truck, grateful there is room for only two people in it.

The drive to the pub is short but Rosie fills it with chatter about the service, the kind words spoken by Margaret, the mourners who had come. I know she is trying to lift me, point out that people care. Her words fill the truck, trying to find a way into my head but they have to compete with the newfound knowledge that Conor had another life in this town, one that I was not part of.

#

When we arrive at the pub Rosie turns to me and takes both of my hands in hers, gently stroking them with her thumbs.

'Now, I know you don't want to do this but it is something that may help. Dismiss your fears, Marianne, these people are here for you.'

I look at her concerned face.

'But I don't know them, Rosie. Who are they? Why do they care?'

'Let's go in and find out. Let them show you.'

She glances at herself in the rear-view mirror, one hand releasing mine to attempt to tame her curly auburn hair, and before I can do the same, opens her door and jumps out. In the brief moment I am alone in the car dread leeches into me, making me nauseous and shivery. As it starts to take hold, the passenger door is wrenched open, letting in the sound of the waves on the beach alongside us, and salty air to freshen my senses.

When Rosie and I enter the pub I sense the chatter inside dying away. I feel a thousand eyes on me, and Rosie's hand on my back, gentle as a kitten, pushing me forward. The pub is gloomy and I can make out only shadows of people as my eyes adjust. Remembering the last time I was here, my steps falter and my eyes dart around in the dim light, looking for safe haven. It is crowded and the two of us jostle our way to a table in the corner. On that night, a lifetime ago, when I had fallen through the same heavy door to see only six men sitting at the bar, it was the vastness of the empty space that petrified me. Today it is the throng of people, the patting of my shoulder, the murmuring of sympathetic words. I have not been in such a multitude of people since leaving university and the rising panic intermingles with feeling like a fraud, an unknown person representing Conor to people he knew and I didn't. Sweat drips down my back and I feel my face flush as I fall into a seat at a corner table with a thin smile. As the sweat cools, my breathing regulates and to my relief I am soon hidden from view as others from the market join the table. The gin and tonic that appears in front of me has warming effects that both dry my sweat and take the edge off my panic. As long as I remain at this table I know I am amongst friends.

The noise in the pub increases as drinks flow and laughter increases. Glimpses between Bert and Colin's shoulders as they lean towards each other, and to Peg and Aoife on either side of them, show me people of all ages crowded around the long bar, seated at high tables in front of it and standing in small groups in any available space. Snatches of conversation drift over.

'Of course, I didn't know him well but he always offered to deliver my shopping home for me.'

'I remember him coming into the shop many times, looking for second-hand bargains. He was always smiling.'

'He asked me if I knew the best place to buy paint. He said he wanted to surprise his wife by painting the bedroom. Lovely man.'

'I met him once, out near the beach He was happy out, walking along whistling. We had a good chat. He was always interested in the farming.'

By my third gin and tonic, the world was more benign. These people were caring and considerate, grateful for the hand of friendship Conor had extended and willing to return it. Maybe the same could be offered to me one day.

It was notable that few came to speak to me. Some had to squeeze past our table on the way to the bathroom and offered an obligatory few words.

'He was a fine fella.'

'I'll always remember his laugh, it was infectious.'

I smiled back at the well-wishers but said nothing. The vacuum inside my head was swirling with questions and tears but no words. I am content to sit with those I know are my friends and absorb the fond feelings for Conor.

'That's her. She drove him away, you know. Had the child alone, the very child of the devil.'

The words punched their way into my hearing, delivered by a tall angular woman, all sharp edges and corners. She was talking to a shorter but no less angular woman as the two of them bustled their way to the bathroom. They would have made a good comedy duo if I felt like laughing. I didn't. I felt like springing across the table and punching them. I flinched as the words hit me, and I jolted the table so that the drinks rocked in the slippery mess of spilt beer and spirits. All those at my table looked at me.

'Are you ok, love?' said Rosie.

'No, I don't think I am. Why do people think they are right? I didn't drive Conor away. Why do they say I did? And who are they to describe Max as the child of the devil. I mean I know he's no angel…'

'Ok, ok. Shall we go? You're probably tired and ready for some peace and quiet. Am I right?' she says.

As the first tears of the day prick my eyes, I nod, and see in the blur Rosie ushering people back from the table to make room for my ungracious exit.

#

In a daze I find myself wrapped in the comforting warmth of Rosie's kitchen, shivering. I can't still my legs or hands and grip my cup of tea hard as I slump in the depths of her battered kitchen sofa. The smell of wet dogs emanates from it, and the warmth they have left behind aids the cosiness. Rosie bustles about making tea, opening and closing cupboard doors, and muttering about 'Those daughters of mine eating the biscuits like they grow on trees.' She finds half a packet of fig rolls, a ginger cake and some oatmeal cookies. 'Of course they don't touch these, the healthy ones with no chocolate,' I hear her mutter as she arranges the selection next to me.

'I can't believe he's gone.'

It is the first thing I am able to say. It's the first time I have said it out loud. Conor is gone. He came back before but he will never come back again. His time at Orchard View was supposed to be in preparation for his return to me, to his real home. I had told him over and over again that Max and I wanted him back to live with us but I was not enough to bring the beauty and joy he spoke of. I had tried, and then I had stopped trying but I had always believed that he would return.

Saying it in the fug of Rosie's kitchen finalised Conor being part of my history but not of my future. I am free and forever imprisoned. With a blood rush of overwhelming guilt I am shocked to feel a trickle of restfulness. It is over.

Chapter 8

Max leaves the house every night now. I don't know where he goes but I hear him returning late at night, fumbling with the key in the door and stumbling around the house. Sometimes he brings friends back with him. Well I don't know whether they are friends, but certainly young men of his age, loud and arrogant, swinging plastic bags containing cans of beer. They stampede downstairs to the kitchen helping themselves to food, and then sit in the drawing room laughing themselves into slumber. Their prone bodies are there in the mornings, fetid alcohol-infused breath creating a fug around the empty bottles and cans dribbling stinking cigarette and roach butts floating in brown slurry onto the scratched floorboards. The boys leave in twos and threes in the late morning, stumbling into daylight and down the drive before Max staggers upstairs without a word to me.

The first time he was brought home by the police I was mortified. A gentle knock on the door at 2am frightened me into wakefulness which turned to horror when I saw Max on the front step being propped up by two Gardai, his eyes slitted, dried blood underneath his nose.

'Sorry to disturb you, Mrs Fairman, but we have brought Max home. We had to break up a fight outside the pub, and he seems to have been involved.'

'Is he ok?' I reach to touch his cheek but shrink back before getting too close, 'What happened?'

'Nothing too serious. No more than a drunken brawl but he needs to keep himself out of this kind of trouble. We can't have this type of mayhem in the town because drink has been taken.'

'Of course not, Gard. Thank you for bringing him back.'

'No trouble at all. I hope this will be the last time.'

But it wasn't. Fights, drugs, petty theft, and vandalism. The Gardai told me each time that knowing my situation they didn't want to have to press charges but if it happened again…

When a victim of Max's aggression threatened to press charges I had one of the most painful and best conversations that I had had with my son for years.

Taking the example from Rosie's kitchen where conversation flows so easily, I make tea and call Max. Scraping back a chair he sits looking at me, defiance blazing in his bloodshot eyes.

'What?'

'I think you know, Max, this can't go on.'

'What can't go on?'

'You, this behaviour, the police bringing you home. That's what can't go on,' my patience snaps, 'You are making enemies all over town, risking a criminal record, not to say your own safety. What is going on?'

'Enemies all over town?' he smirked, 'As if we didn't already have those after what you have put us through. I could make people like me if I wanted to but I don't. I don't care. I am not here to be liked. I am here to succeed. I just have to find a way.'

I remain quiet, hearing only his accusation of 'all that I had put us through' echoing around my head.

'I've spent all my life behind these iron gates of this monstrosity of a house. Oh yes, I did make a brief foray into the world when I was a small child. You pushed me out there and I hated it. All those people wanting different things of me. Be good, be kind, be nice. Well why should I? I never felt like I belonged with them. Never felt like I was one of them. I am not good or kind or nice. Don't see the point. I knew then that they looked at me differently, as though they knew I didn't belong, and they still do. Well I don't want to belong to their small, boring world. I will show them all one day how different I am.'

'You never told me you feel this way, Max.'

'How could I have told you? I know you resent me for not being Conor. Nothing I say can change that, so I say nothing. And neither do you. We live separately and we always have done. You didn't want me and I don't want you.'

His black eyes bore into me, full of hate and hurt. My own fill with tears. He is right. I do resent him for not being Conor.

'And I certainly didn't belong to that man who you called my father. He never once called himself my father, only you did that. He just stared at me. Or shouted at me. When he left the first time I wasn't even here but when he came back I was. Do you remember that, Mother? I WAS HERE. I know you would have preferred it if I wasn't but I was.'

His words bounce around the kitchen hitting me with greater force on each rebound.

'You held on for so long to the ridiculous idea that the house is the legacy of that man, but having him in the house didn't work for anyone. You said he wasn't the same as he had been. Well how do I know that's true? All I do know is that when he was here I felt even more like I didn't belong, not even in the house I was growing up in.'

With those words I almost hear my heart snapping. Looking at this raging young man seeing the anger in his tight lips, bright eyes, clenched hands, holding together a thin membrane around sadness and loss that has threatened him all of his life, I have never felt such a failure.

'Max,' my voice is low, husky, 'I wish I had done more to help you but I didn't know how to. I am your mother…'

'My mother?' he snapped back. 'My mother? You have never felt like my mother, and face it, you didn't want to be my mother. I am not the child that you wanted.'

'That is not true, Max. I longed for a child. I was so happy when you were born'

'A child yes, but not me as that child. I know, Mother, I know.'

Are his eyes filling up? I can hardly bear anymore of this, and with his next words, I don't have to.

'Anyway, it's over now, Mother. I'll be up and out in the morning.'

'What do you mean?' I stutter, the two halves of my heart reaching for each other with a tightness in my chest that leaves me gasping for breath. Is he leaving?

'I've got a job haven't I. Need to make some money so I can get out of this place for once and for all.'

I stare at him as he throws himself out of the chair and out of the room, leaving me aching with the fantasies of what might have been, and the memories of what has gone.

#

Max has a job as a labourer with Cronin's construction firm, and for the next few months he leaves the house by 6.00 every morning, returning late in the evenings, drunk and seeking his bed. We hardly see each other and never speak. I leave dinner for him every night and it is gone in the mornings, dirty plates scattered on the table.

The new routine brings a restfulness for me. Max wants nothing more from me than meals and cupboards of food and beer, easy for me to provide with my income from the market. With this new absence and the permanence of Conor's I am free to reinvent myself. I am no longer either a wife or a mother. I can bury my pain.

It is Rosie's idea that we start going for walks together.

'I need to lose weight and get fit,' she says one day, squeezing and pummelling her bulging midriff. 'Since my Maria has got into baking, there are always too many cakes around the place. Talking of which I brought treacle cake,' she proffers me a plate with a slice of cake on it the size of a doorstop. I take it of course.

'I know! Let's go power-walking,' she says, marching around the kitchen, exaggerating high swings of her arms, legs striding across the slate-tiled floor. 'We can bring Jessie too,' she laughs as she bends to pat the ancient farm collie who is enjoying her days of retirement lounging on the sofa being stroked.

I think it's a great idea. An excuse to get out of the house, and spend more time with Rosie whose company is the best I know.

We start the next day, meeting at the gates to my house, both wearing tattered trainers and tracksuits, hair tied back and faces shining with anticipation.

Rosie is not fit. Our walk is broken by dramatic halts for breath as she bends over clasping her knees, hands on hips, gasping in lungfuls of air. The few cars that pass beep cheery hellos to Rosie as we stride, and our breathless conversation covers local gossip, and a hilarious story of her daughter's attempts to sneak back into the house at 3am, not knowing she is being watched by Rosie and Jessie as she struggles through a tiny window.

When we part, back at the gates, I skip up the drive, adrenaline fuelled. Within ten minutes I am fast asleep in the armchair, an undrunk cup of dark-brown Barry's tea cooling on the table beside me.

Our walks become part of a new daily routine. Early morning swim, followed by some sewing or jewellery-making before meeting Rosie mid-morning at the gates, and off we go. After two weeks she is already fitter and we venture onto new and longer routes, following unmade tracks over the top of rocky hills with breath-taking views, or untrodden paths around hidden loughs and reedy lakes.

Today I am going to suggest that we veer right at the bend beyond the beach and see where it takes us. Always willing to find new territory, Rosie agrees.

In the bright peacefulness of the valley, and in a rare moment of silence between us, we hear only the lowing of cattle and twittering of birds as we stride, arms swinging, as we breathe in the freshness. The hills look down on us as we walk, proud and protective. The sky has cleared to a dull grey that manages to send down shafts of sun in between enveloping coolness. We exchange half-smiles when we catch each other's eyes, and peace infuses us both.

The sound of several cars approaching is intrusive. Rosie and I hurtle ourselves into the ditches on either side of the road as three cars round the bend and race past us, leaving in their wake trails of black fumes.

'What the bloody hell...' says Rosie, as we step back onto the road with caution.

As the cars pull into a field up ahead Rosie and I glance at each other. We hasten towards a fuchsia bush that shields us from the view of the group of six men who have stepped out of the cars, and strain to listen to their conversation.

Dressed in heavy boots and bright yellow hard hats framing drab grey suits, the men look out of place in the vast emptiness of greenery. They introduce themselves to each other in city accents, pointing and waving at the overgrown expanse of land whilst a couple of them make notes on clipboards.

'So we are planning on twenty-seven houses in a horseshoe shape,' says one.

'Twenty-seven?' responds another. 'We can bump that up to thirty if you reduce the size of the gardens.'

'Grand, let's do that. That will bring us more profit,' comes the retort.

Rosie and I look at each other, mouths open, eyebrows raised, as the conversation continues

'The types who live in these houses won't value gardens anyway. They'll only go outside to go to the pub or the bingo, and the smaller their garden the less likely they are to raise their vicious dogs and scrawny horses here.'

Rosie hurrumphs so loudly that I worry we might be heard. I press my finger to my lips and urge her with my eyes to stay quiet and hidden. She clutches her hand to her mouth to gag herself and her eyes above it look even larger. Two of the men have started to walk around the edge of the field, spraying ugly white lines on the coarse grass and gorse where the other four point and gesticulate. Rosie and I can't help smirking when the shouted communication is thwarted by a sharp wind that has blown up from nowhere.

'Mark that spot for the septic tanks,' one calls out.

'What?' comes the response from another, who cups one ear and leans towards him.

'The septic tanks, mark the spot.'

The show becomes comical as the men start wrapping their thin suit jackets around them, shouting misheard instructions to each other to try and overcome the whining of the wind. The rattle of the dry brown leaves adds to the communication challenge and with heads bent as they graffiti the field, the group looks like a most unlikely herd of animals reaching for grass. When one of the men in the centre slips in the mud running down to a stream, events take a turn.

'For feck's sake,' he says, sliding more as he tries to stand up, before accepting a helping hand from a colleague. 'This will either have to be blocked or diverted,' he says, jerking one hand towards the stream whilst trying to brush the mud from his clothes.

'Maybe we can find the source and use that to supply the water to the houses?' another suggests, scattering sweet wrappers from his pocket as he reaches in for a pen. 'It might save money.'

Heads turn to follow the course of the stream to a large mound occupying the centre of the land.

'That's going to have to be flattened. We can direct water from to supply the main pipes.'

I felt Rosie shaking with another angry hurrumph as she whispers, 'They'll have the wrath of the fairies to deal with if they do. That's a fairy mound.'

By the time the men have sprayed large white crosses on several trees the short sharp gusts of wind have whipped up into a biting gale that smacks at the men's faces, Well-prepared in our thick waterproof coats we watch as stinging rain comes in sideways to spit with icy tongues at the men's faces. They slip and slide back up the field with gorse thorns whipping at their ankles.

'Why anyone would want to live in this godforsaken place with its wild weather I don't know,' says one of the men.

'But there's always someone who will,' says another. 'We'll probably be able to sell off-plan. Let's get out of here, I've seen enough. Let's go back to the office and cost up.'

Rosie and I press ourselves into the bushes as the cars move out of their mud pools, splattering the hedgerows with brown sludge and tainting the air with exhaust fumes. The moment their cars are out of sight, a calm falls over the land again, the trees still as the birds sing a joyful farewell.

#

Two days later is market day again. Pulling our tables together we sit cupping our coffee.

'I can't stop thinking about it, Rosie,' I begin. 'It was so shocking to hear those men's contempt for the land.'

'I know. We might have to get a campaign up to stop the development,' she says, a determined look in her eye, 'if the fairies don't do it for us.'

'The fairies? Oh come on'

To my amazement Rosie shuffles in her seat, averting her eyes from mine.

'Weeeelll, I don't believe in them, but I know that they're there,' she half-smiles before assuming a serious face. 'But then again, look at how successful they were in driving the men away.'

'You are messing with me, you don't think that was fairies do you?' I reply. 'That was just a squall, the weather playing up as usual.'

'I know I know, but it succeeded in making short shrift of those men didn't it? Don't you think it is a bit of a coincidence, springing up just as they were talking about flattening the fairy hill?'

I find myself contemplating the possibility. I had heard mutterings for all my life about a parallel world of little folk, *sidhe*, living alongside us. Great Aunt Alice had no time for the fairies. To her, everyone's fate is predetermined according to God's will. To even talk about fairies was an insult, but I had heard whispers about the importance of the fairies protecting livestock, of fairy forts left alone to avoid the fairies' vengeance, and fairy paths left clear for the annual fairy trooping. Sometimes, with horror in the voice of the narrator, I heard of unexplained accidents and deaths of those who offended the fairies As a child the stories were nothing more than distractions from the dullness of schooldays. There was certainly no evidence of fairy influence in the grey-walled convent where we were taught to learn by rote and endless repetition. Now though, I remember how Rosie had hushed Cathleen with vehemence when she had suggested to me that Conor had been taken by fairies. I am intrigued when she says in a soft voice

'My mother swears that our father was taken by them.'

Rosie has never talked about her parents before. I assumed that they had both died but it was unclear why she, the girl and the third-born of her siblings, was living in the family house and running the farm. I don't need to say anything. Rosie's glance around the near-empty market for potential customers and the way she settles herself into her fold-up chair tells me that I will hear her story. With a thrill of excitement I follow suit and wriggle my bottom into a more comfortable position.

'It was a normal evening in the winter of 1978. I was fifteen. Mam had made the tea, I remember to this day that it was lamb chops with mashed potatoes, peas and carrots, and the four of us had sat down with Da, Mam still bustling around. It was the usual banter of me being teased by my brothers and my Da laughing until he left to milk the cows. That's what happened every day. Da would leave and the three of us would help clear away until Mam hustled us out of the kitchen telling us we were getting in her way and didn't we have any schoolwork to do. That day I remember Da giving my hair a stroke as he passed me on the way to the back door where his boots were. I was still eating and hardly responded.'

Her eyes cloud for a minute, before she resumes.

'Afterwards the three of us went upstairs to our bedrooms. I think John and Patrick went together to read their football magasines in Patrick's room but I went to mine and lay on my bed looking at my Jackie magazine. I heard Da's jeep driving away and up the lane to the milking parlour. It was dark by then and the weather was raging. It was winter, otherwise he would have walked.

'The evening passed as usual. I lay on my bed pretending to do my homework until Mam called up that it was time for bed. It seemed like hours later but it must have been only about midnight that I was woken by shouting and the glare from car headlights swinging into my room. Peeping out of my curtains I saw neighbours driving up to the house, talking in low voices in our front yard. Of course I went downstairs, still in my pyjamas, and found Mam in the kitchen on her own, sort of pacing around, and fiddling with saucepans and the like. When Patrick, and John were there too she told us that Da hadn't come home so our friends were going out looking for him. I remember it becoming so quiet after the neighbours drove off. I was in the kitchen with Ma just waiting for Da or some news.'

Rosie's eyes spilled tears now.

'He never came back. No one has seen him from then to now. They searched everywhere, the Cliff Rescue came out and looked along the cliffs, we all searched the ditches for days after. Nothing. It's a complete mystery. Ma became convinced he had been taken by the fairies. She says it's the only explanation. The parlour was new you see and he had tried to shift a fairy rock with his digger to make room for it. It was impossible to move so he built it a few feet along but Mam thought he must have angered them by tampering with their home. She went to her grave believing that was what happened.'

My heart pumps blood straight to my head. I can hear it coursing in my ears. I want so much to show Rosie compassion, to be for her in this moment what she has been to me in my dark times but my resolve falters as I think only of my own loss. Unexplained and unsolved. Conor too had disappeared without a trace. To suggest it was fairies that took him seems nonsensical yet the world he talked of on his return could have been a fairy world. Is it possible that Rosie and I share the same grief of unexplained loss?

As I muse, Rosie sits upright and declares, 'Of course it's nonsense. He must have fallen over a hedge somewhere and lain there undiscovered until he died. It's happened before. All I know is that from that day I took over running the farm with Ma. When my brothers were old enough they scarpered. They said there was a curse on the place and didn't want anything to do with it. Went to England to work on the building sites, both of them.'

She sniffs several times and brushes a hand across her eyes, looking at me for reassurance. I do my best.

Something about Rosie's story resonates within me though and settles in the recesses of my mind.

'Do you have catnip?'

Our thoughts are broken by a customer and we both start bustling about, Rosie serving her customer, me rearranging my jewellery in a needless way.

#

For weeks after this conversation I imagined I could see lights in the woods again, hear music on the breeze in the garden. One day I lost the keys to the car and found myself wondering whether mischievous fairies had moved them in retaliation for a careless misdemeanour of mine. When I found them again, in a coat pocket, I remembered that I had left them there the day before. I scolded myself for being so silly and dismissed the intrusions as effects of grief.

Nonetheless, possibilities of Conor being taken by fairies crept into my head. It provided an explanation for the mystery, for his talk of another world. Reasoning with myself, I reminded myself that it was nonsense, that I agreed with Rosie. How could big strong men like Conor and Rosie's father be taken away by fairies? And anyway, Conor had come back. He had returned, albeit a different and broken man. Surely that other world he spoke of couldn't have been where the fairies lived?

Just when I thought I had rid myself of such unhelpful thoughts I heard about a tragedy that revived them all. *Young Man Killed at Local Beauty Spot*. My morbid fascination drew me to read the article in the local newspaper.

The family of Donal O'Brien (17) are mourning his loss after a tragic accident at the site he was helping to prepare for the much objected-to housing development project. Details are still emerging but it appears that the branch of a tree fell on the van he was in, crushing him to death. The foreman, Max Fairman, said 'How this accident happened is beyond our understanding and investigations are starting immediately. We send our deepest condolences to the O'Brien family on their loss.'

Reading of Max's involvement in the tragic accident at the very place where Rosie and I had eavesdropped sent a shockwave through me.

Since plans for the development at the site have been made public there has been much local campaigning to halt them. The site has long been used by walkers and families as a local recreation and beauty spot, and it is unclear how planning permission was obtained to build on it. One local campaigner who wishes to remain anonymous has told this newspaper, "There is something fishy about this development. The papers applying for planning permission seem to have disappeared and no one at the council is taking responsibility for this. For this tragedy to happen only underlines our concern and we will now redouble our efforts to halt work there immediately."

I breathe heavily as I try to think this through. Max has made no mention of the tragedy nor of his promotion to foreman. I fear for how he will be perceived by the locals now that this had happened on his watch. It is painful to imagine what the O'Brien family is going through. Their lost son was three years younger than my own. I cannot sit with the deep sorrow I feel and snatching up my anorak I rush over to Rosie's house.

#

As ever the key is in the lock of her front door and I turn and push in one movement, calling out.

'Rosie, have you heard? Have you seen the paper?'

Rosie is at her kitchen table, head in hands, reading glasses on, with the paper spread open in front of her.

'Yes, I'm just reading it now. I'm the anonymous source. I only spoke to them last night and they've printed it already. It's a terrible thing to happen. Poor Peggy, to lose her youngest this way.'

'It says something about a tree branch falling on the van.' I say, 'But how could that happen? There hasn't been a breath of wind for days. Was there a dead tree there?'

'Heaven only knows… oh.'

We both turn at the sound of the kitchen door opening to see a woman, hair pulled back into a messy ponytail, long black skirt and green jumper, and eyes sunk into black rings. She stands at the door looking at us, hesitant to enter.

'Peggy, love, come in, sit down.'

Rosie jumps up to guide the woman to a chair. She has to almost push her onto it because Peggy is in such a trance that even this small movement is nearly beyond her.

'Marianne, this is Donal O'Brien's mam, Peggy. What can I get you love, have a cup of tea.'

'I am so sorry for your loss, Mrs O'Brien,' I whisper, feeling useless and relying on Rosie to handle the situation. She does of course, allowing the three of us to sit in silence until Peggy starts to speak in a voice so low that Rosie and I shuffle towards her in our chairs to hear.

'They can't understand it. The wind came from nowhere. He was making tea in the van. The rest of them were in the field. They just heard the crash. Tommy Óg went running to him but it was too late. Nothing they could do.'

Her staccato speech belied her incredulity at what had happened, but Rosie and I looked at each other over Peggy's head. We both remembered the sudden change in the weather that we too had witnessed at that site only a few weeks before. It must be because it is unprotected, on top of a hill, vulnerable to the gusts coming off the ocean. Surely nothing to do with fairies? I had a host of questions running round my head: Was he not wearing a hard hat? Why was he making tea inside a van? and a niggling worry 'Where was Max, the foreman whose job it was to ensure the safety of the work crew?'

The full details unfolded over the days that followed, gaps filled in by Brendan, a close friend of Tommy Óg, Peggy's eldest son. The four-man crew had arrived at the site early in the morning, to make up for lost time the day before when work had been abandoned because of a thick mist that had rolled in. The digger machines were due that day and the preparation of the site needed to be completed. From the moment the crew arrived the weather was foul, squalls of heavy rain followed by gales that howled around the men as they tried to stake out the land for the diggers. Donal had been brought along at the last minute because Michael, the middle of Peggy's sons, had called in sick.

The weather had made them all bad-tempered and when Sean, the other member of the crew had fallen into the stream, Sean had yelled to Donal to get a brew on. Not knowing whether to carry on with the rock clearing of the boundaries that Max had asked him to do, or to go back and make tea, Donal had gone looking for Max. In the next twenty minutes the weather had worsened. The squalls turned into a persistent shower of icy needles blown sideways by ferocious wind that did battle with the trees on its way across the field. Grumpy enough, Brendan, Sean and Cian had assumed that Donal had taken shelter and decided to do the same, moving into the trees hoping for calm. They had not seen Max in all this time and thought he must be in his car at the entrance to the field.

Sean had got impatient waiting for Donal and was trying to light the small gas stove behind the van, to little avail. When Donal reappeared, complaining of having got lost, Sean had roared at him to bloody well sort it out, before jumping down and going to find the others. Donal, left on his own, must have decided to take the stove into the van to light it, and was inside when a massive branch broke off and crushed it. The men, waiting underneath the trees, said he hadn't stood a chance.

The O'Briens were an established family in the area, with a long history of house building and construction.

Tommy O'Brien senior, Tommy Mór, owned the tool hire company in the town, supplying contactors for miles around. Donal's older brothers, Tommy óg and Michael, were working out their apprenticeships as labourers before joining their father in the business. It was expected that Donal would have done the same.

Everybody knew the family and the steady stream of condolences were evident all around the town, a special Mass was said for Donal, many flowers were at the entrance to the accursed field and people wore black armbands around town in remembrance of him.

In the passing contact I had with Max in the days that followed, he never mentioned the tragedy. He was in a temper more foul than I had ever seen and snapped me into silence when I tried to broach it with him. It was his first job in charge and I concluded the feelings must be hard for him, but not ones he was going to share. How wrong I was.

#

The wake, held at the O'Briens' house, saw traffic jams blocking the roads. On Rosie's advice I went along to the house to pay my respects. I was reluctant, not knowing how I would be received by the grieving family but Rosie said that it was important. I was pleased that she came with me. Peggy's gentleness pervaded the whole family. As I arrived at the house, which had been scrubbed inside and out, and walked in past plates of sandwiches and drinks laid out on tables, I saw Peggy at the other side of the room. She was flanked by her husband and two remaining sons. I manoeuvred my way through the crowd to her, shaking and clammy but determined to offer my sympathies. She saw me over the heads of the crowd and reached her hand out to me. A warmth ran through me as I grasped it with both of mine in gratitude.

'This is Mrs Fairman,' she said.

I saw a look of anger flash across Tommy Óg's face, but he suppressed it and nodded to me. Michael didn't look at me as Mr O'Brien reached out a large, coarse hand to take one of mine.

'You are welcome in our house, Mrs Fairman. We appreciate you taking the time.' His voice was hoarse and low.

'Please have a drink, have a sandwich,' said Peggy, waving her hands at the spread before turning to the next mourner. With relief I backed away and turned to look for Rosie.

Wandering through the crowd I heard hushed snatches of conversation; 'tragedy', 'senseless waste' but also, 'someone should be accountable', and 'why was no one looking out for the lad?' spoken in more strident demanding voices. As I reached for a glass of wine from the table I heard more detail.

'Of course, Michael wasn't there on the day. Can you imagine how he feels?' a woman of about my age, wearing a black skirt and grey blouse, that managed to look much more appropriate than my slightly shabby black dress bought yesterday at the second-hand shop.

I had to strain to hear the response from her companion, a woman with hair that was so tight with curls that it didn't move.

'You know why don't you? He heard the banshee. The O'Brien banshee. It kept him up all night so he called in sick in the morning.'

Her friend gasped, clutching a hand with rings tightly fitted around chubby fingers to her mouth.

'No? Heralding a death, and it was his own brother's death it was foretelling. How terrible.'

I was struck by the matter of fact way in which this news had been imparted and received. The harbingers of death, the banshees, were said to belong to very few families, but when they were heard a member of that family would die. It seemed to be becoming the explanation for the death of young Donal.

#

The funeral the next day was a town affair. Everybody turned out. The streets lined with mourners were silent as the hearse made its way to the town's cathedral, larger and grander than the small chapel in which Conor's service had been held. Inside, the occasional sob cut through the incense-scented air, muffled only by the density of human bodies that filled every pew. The family's grief was palpable in their erect figures seated at the front, paying their final respects to a beloved brother. Donal was the youngest child, the cheekiest boy and the one who got away with the most mischief. He was doted on by his mother and protected by his older brothers who had started including him in their own hijinks as he came of age. The priest's eulogy was touching, acknowledging that Donal's death seemed senseless and that this made it all the harder to bear. He spoke softly of how much he was loved, with words that echoed above the anguish that impregnated the high vaults, and remained there long after the coffin had left the building.

Feeling the atmosphere, seeing the statues, staring down from crucifixes, cradling babies, or clutching wounds of martyrdom, stirred up long-forgotten emotions of confusion for me. No higher force had done anything to let me be brought up in the comfort of parental love, or to protect me from tragedy upon tragedy in my life as a mother and wife, now widow. I could not believe in its existence. It was easier for me to accept that there were banshees and fairies than that there was a god. I was uncomfortable but knew it was important to be seen there, particularly as once again there was no sign of Max.

Tommy Óg, Michael, and Mr O'Brien, along with Brendan, were the pall bearers. Heads held high, their pride in Donal was tangible. The sun's brilliance during the burial was ever after spoken off as a sign of the affection held for him. The same force of nature that had caused his death seemed to put on a display of light for his burial, and the crowd gasped when a butterfly appeared and flitted around the coffin before it was lowered into the ground.

'That's the poor boy's soul,' echoed in whispers around the church.

The family had put money behind the bar at the pub for the reception afterwards. The crowd was larger than it had been for Conor's funeral. People were spilling out of the door as toast after toast was made to Donal and his family.

'To the finest lad dealt the cruellest blow.'

'To the O'Brien family, who have gained an angel today.'

'To Donal O'Brien, gone but never to be forgotten.'

Sitting with Rosie and the others from the market at the same beer-stained table in the corner where we had sat at after Conor's cremation, I watched love and respect pour from people's hearts to the family. Stories were told as reminiscing started, but it was when the singing began that I felt tears collecting in my eyes. Haunting 'Danny Boy' of course but also the 'Fields of Athenry' in recognition of his love for the Irish Rugby team. When his gorgeous young girlfriend stood and sang 'Nothing Compares to You', a thrill trembled through the crowd and I was not alone in my tears.

I cannot help thinking of Conor as I absorb the atmosphere. It feels as though he is here with me as I strive to show the respect that our absent son does not. It is as the owner of the pub is calling for hush to make an announcement that I see Max coming in to the pub. I am relieved. Now he too can offer condolences, mourn the loss with the community, acknowledge some responsibility. I see him waiting by the door until the end of the announcement that an annual memorial walk will be held in memory of Donal, to raise money for charity. As the chatter starts up again, I wave to try and attract his attention, but he does not see me as he scans the pub, looking intent on finding someone. When I see him making his way to Brendan I feel a flutter of pride thinking he is at last going to do the right thing. To my horror, within minutes of the two meeting, Brendan has punched Max, flooring him. The crowd has backed away in silence, watching Max and holding Brendan back. No one offers to help Max up.

'No, I fecking well will not be back at work tomorrow, you unfeeling git. In fact I will not come back and work for you ever again. I quit.' Brendan roars at Max, 'How dare you disrespect the memory of Donal. You didn't take care of him in life and you don't care about him in death. Well you and your new houses can feck off.'

With a final humiliating stab at him Brendan says, 'And by the way, I know that you are in the pay of the developers, so,' he turns to the crowd, 'does anyone want to work for this man so that he can fleece others with shoddy houses whilst lining his own pockets?'

The crowd thunders back as one, 'No, feck off Fairman', and I have to watch them bundle my son out of the door into the cold night. Rosie touches me on the hand and flicks her eyes to the back door.

'I think we should go, love,' and the two of us wave discreet goodbyes to the other market traders as we sidle out.

#

Time has done little to heal how the townsfolk feel about Donal's death. There are stories of the greed of the management of the proposed development, of Max's negligence on the day, of corner-cutting, and of carelessness. Even poor Michael attracted some disapproval for not having been there and being the reason why Donal had gone to work that day. Tommy Óg hid away, perhaps wrestling with guilt about not having protected his brother from this most awful of events. There was no point and no need for anyone to try and defend themselves, but it embarrasses me that Max makes no effort to reconcile with the community. He stays at home much more and never speaks to me. Hiding away like a coward I assume. I leave him to it.

The afternoons when Peggy appears at Rosie's house are painful, joining us for tea but not able to talk about anything other than the loss of her son. She is desperate to recount all that she can about Donal's last day and how his death ended it.

Michael had told her that Tommy Óg had offered to take Donal and the rest of the crew for a drink after work to thank them for pitching in for him. He told his mother that when Donal had complained about being bitten by midges around the stream the men had teased him and told him he wasn't ready for a working man's world yet. Brendan had told her how Donal reminded him of his own son at that age and that he had resolved to look out for him, and how bad he felt that he hadn't been able to. She wants to hear from Rosie and me of any other titbits of information she can add to help her understand how or why this accident happened, to help her with her grief. She wants to keep the memory of her son close to her heart, and sucks in the love for Donal that others have, to join her own.

Her grief was not only for herself. She worried about the impact of the loss of Donal on her other boys. Tommy Óg had always kept a keen eye on his younger sibling. Her eldest child was developing his own life successfully and had been the child Peggy had worried about the least, until now. She told us that now he comes to her house most days, talking of disappointment, helplessness. She worried when he resigned his job. She had looked forward to the time when he would be elevated to a senior position within the family company, but now he shows no interest in working at all, relying on his wife's salary to keep them both, and blaming himself for what happened to Donal.

A small consolation to Peggy was that Donal's death had provoked a new openness in Michael. This brother spoke to her about how he felt, most often in relation to losing his youngest brother, but also in relation to his life and his future. He spoke of his longing to see Donal again, of what he would have said to him. He told her also that he hardly slept now, reliving the dreadful banshee wailing that had kept him awake in the night before the day of Donal's death, and about how he walks the town for hours at night seeking respite from the turmoil of his feelings. She can only tell him that at least there is comfort in knowing that the banshee has accompanied Donal safely to the other side.

With this, and through her agony, Peggy found an explanation for Donal's death. Violent weather, sudden blinding mists descending, men getting lost in fields... She had heard of such things before in the stories told around living room fires. Her thoughts whirled around in her head until they organised themselves into some sense to help her live with this new tragedy in her life. With the acceptance that Michael's distress had been caused by the banshee came a new peace for Peggy. She understood the strange happenings in the field as being caused by the fairy folk. They must have had a reason to see off the humans and their plans for development, and to Peggy, Tommy Óg's decision to have nothing more to do with it came to be the correct one. I wondered if she tried to suppress thoughts that it should have been Max Fairman that was taken and not her precious boy, as she see-sawed between her beliefs in fairies and in God's mysterious ways, to comfort herself.

#

The contractors never came back, and in the weeks after Donal's death the field restored itself to its former natural state with no indication of the fatality that had occurred there, until Peggy took to placing flowers at the spot where the van had been crushed.

Every time she visits she casts her eyes around for signs of fairy folk. She knows the hill is the place where they live, and the beauty of the field and its surrounding pastures is part of their kingdom. She knows they do not object to the laying of flowers, and sometimes thinks she sees a glint of fairy tokens, special shells or beautiful stones, lying in the grass amongst them. She never takes them away but always thanks the fairies out loud for taking care of her poor boy's death site.

Chapter 9

The bang of the front door shatters the still silence of the house. Max is shouting for me. I am surprised because his visits are rare now that the building company has supplied him with a luxury apartment in the city. Placing the quilt I am working on over the arms of the chair, I stand up to smooth down my skirt, and tuck stray hairs behind my ear, taking my time before stepping out of my studio. Since he moved out it has become easier and easier not to rush to meet Max's every demand but nonetheless a small shiver of trepidation ripples its way down my spine.

'Mother, I need to talk to you. Come in here.'

Max is striding towards the drawing room, calling over his shoulder, confident that I will follow as I emerge into the hallway.

Pavlov, the room Max had commandeered when he lived here, is still cluttered with his books and papers. His commands to me not to touch anything when he moved out left me with no desire to do so, and the door has remained closed ever since.

He is seated on the sofa, legs splayed, eyes shining, urgency radiating from his face.

'So, I need a new project. There is a gap in the schedule at work and if I can fill it, I'm bound to get promoted again. It will take me to senior management level.'

He looks at me, not for affirmation, not with apology, but with expectation of reciprocal excitement. I can't feel it. I want to, but only feel concern. My spine heats my back, flicking flames of fire up it. I no longer know what lengths my son will go to in pursuit of his ascension to a status he feels he is entitled to.

'You know I can't get anyone from round here to work for me since that business with the lad, but if I find the right site I can bring some more fellas down from the city.

The developers have been looking for a place round here for years. It's an ideal spot what with the town, the sea, the road connections.'

He pauses.

'And I have found it.'

This time his look is one of triumph. I feel the fire roil into dread deep in my stomach. It threatens to rise to my face but I compose my appearance to one of interest

'Ok,' I say with a hesitation that I hope doesn't show. 'Where is it?''

Misreading my acting as sincere he continues with excitement. 'It needs to be big enough for twenty-five or thirty houses, close to town but with countryside around, near a road but not on a road. We're thinking young families, professionals, first-time buyers, people who want to get on the property ladder at an affordable price.'

The intensity of his gaze tells me he expects me to have figured out where he is talking about, but I see the land in which I live as opportunity for walks and peace, not as potential building sites. I return his look, waiting for more.

'Here, Mother, here'

It takes me a moment.

'Here? What do you mean here?'

'Here. Our land. The land around the house. Hell, the house itself, we can divide it up into apartments, and sell them at a premium. We'll build separate houses all around. It's perfect. It's got everything. You can have the penthouse if you like.'

The cauldron in my stomach turns into an engulfing black anger that brings with it a clarity that brooks no argument.

'No, Max, no. Absolutely not. My land is not for sale.'

He smiles. 'It's ok, Mother, I am not suggesting I buy it, just build on it. I'm going to…'

'You are not going to build on it. You are not going to buy it. You are not going to have anything to do with ruining this land. My land.'

121

Shaking, I stop my words and give in to my urge to get far away from my grabbing, thoughtless son. I stride out to the hallway and through the front door, left open by him in his hurry to ruin my life. I breathe fresh air in through my nose and out through my mouth, trying to quell the stampede of emotions. I march towards the lawn, arms rigid and swinging, head filled with a kaleidoscope of images of Conor, the house, the woods, the meadows, blurring and whirling into ugly rows of house. I want to put distance between me and Max, afraid of what I might say if I do not. I am disgusted by his proposal, his callousness in wanting to destroy our home, its environment, the Context. Max sees it only as an opportunity for financial gain with no thought for my wishes. I see it as a retreat, a sanctuary, the place that saved me from collapse into hopelessness. How could he ever have imagined I would agree to dig it up for houses to be built on it?

I reach the lake and, breathing fast, rip off my clothes to splash through the reeds in my underwear, and throw myself into the caress of the water. I head to its centre, looking through the shimmer of the water to the hills beyond, seeking the peace and calm they always bring me.

I swim first with a franticness that sends the moorhens and heron flapping away in agitation, but after a while I settle into smooth, languid strokes that hardly break the surface. I stop often, treading water, inhaling its scent, feeling its embrace, and staring at the lush green vastness that surrounds me. As my breathing slows and evens out, my stomach stretches into a containing tautness, my arms support me as my feet paddle, and I am one with the water. My mind is still and blank and brings the relief I have sought.

When cold starts to penetrate I head for the shore, ignorant of how long I have been swimming but noticing the gloom of evening making shadows of the trees. Rubbing myself dry with my clothes, not caring about the mud that smears me and them, thoughts of Max re-enter my mind. I hope he has gone from the house. I do not want to encounter him or be reminded of what has passed between us.

I walk back slowly, relishing the fresh clean feel of my body, fearing what I will find. As I take in the darkening shadows of the trees and hills my mind feels cleansed but alert. I pick lavender sprigs from the lush cerulean bush in front of the house and hold them to my nose as I pass through the front door and start up the stairs.

'So, have you had time to think?'

I whirl round. He is standing there, arrogant and ignorant. I throw the lavender sprig at him.

'Out, out, get out of my house,'.

My hand balls into a fist and I fight to keep it by my side.

'I have done everything for you. I have given you every last ounce of what I have. I have sacrificed more than you will ever know to give you what you wanted. And what has happened? I have created a monster. You are a monster, Max. Everybody else has seen it and now I see it for myself. Well no more, that's it. It's over. You are a selfish, uncaring, greedy man and you are no longer welcome in my house. Ever. Now go.'

The thrill of seeing him shocked elates me. It is what I want. To give him a kick in the teeth, to devastate him. I wanted to pierce that armour of coldness that surrounds him, and I succeeded. His dark eyes are wide with disbelief before he turns and runs from my rage, saying nothing. I run to slam the door behind him, panting with victory.

Slumping with my back against the door, the heat of my rage glows and softens the tension in my body. I am amazed at myself. Those words came from deep inside me, unbidden but welcome. They are all the silenced retorts and attacks held back for years, and today, with his proposal, it is as though all the forces that have rested within me for so long, mustered themselves into a triumphant charge that leaves me weak. No doubt Max will think that I will acquiesce but no, not this time. I am not prepared to relinquish my last link with the life I started with Conor. I have learnt enough from Rosie and the others to know that I don't have to put up with his bullying, and they have given me the strength to resist him. This time I will stand firm against him, over and over if needs be. With my last trickles of strength, I pour myself two fingers of Jameson to take with me upstairs to bed.

#

My confrontation with Max exhausted me and I managed to sleep through the whole night. My dreams alternated between peaceful tropical wanderings, and panicked running from rainstorms and clouds, but when I wake today I feel rested, knowing that I am correct in forbidding my greedy-eyed son him from returning to the house he wishes to destroy.

As the morning progresses from dim half-light to full sun, niggles of guilt begin to nibble at my insides. I keep reliving the argument, picturing Max's face contorted into menacing anger. I hear my words screamed at him in a way he has never experienced before, harsh, assertive. No wonder he looked so surprised. My anger returns now. For him to trample over my feelings in the way he did…I need to get out of the house. These replays are eating me up. I head for distraction and comfort.

Walking through her front door I hear Rosie talking to someone. I expect it may be Peggy or another of her regular visitors but from the doorway of the kitchen I see someone I don't know. She is a young woman with a body that clothes designers would call 'petite'. Her small pointed face is pale and so clear that it appears almost translucent, framed with long strawberry blonde hair that falls to her shoulders in soft curls. She is looking down at her small white hands and they are fidgeting with each other, distracting me from the dress printed with dozens of tiny pink flowers that falls in folds to the floor. Struck by her attractiveness I am lost for words. Rosie is at the Aga, chattering away, her ruddy face and broad hands streaked with flour. She uses the back of a hand to wipe the sweat from her forehead, streaking it white as she ushers me in.

'Marianne, sweetie, come in. I just made banana cake and the kettle's just boiled. Perfect timing.'

I sit on the hard-backed chair next to the stranger, my anger receded into curiosity but feeling the tension that has taken hold of my body.

'This is Bella. I found her wandering on the road outside. She's looking for someone. A family member or something. She's only just arrived in town, from… well I don't know where you're from dear, but you're very welcome, isn't she Marianne?'

'Of course, hi. I live down the road,' I raise a hand to offer to shake hers. Bella looks hesitant but gives me a shy smile.

'Hello, very pleased to meet you,' she says in a formal manner that exacerbates her nervousness.

I give her my best welcoming-face, and pull out a chair for Rosie as she joins us with tea and banana cake. This is a welcome distraction from the turmoil in my head, and I cast my eyes up and down Bella's trim figure, admiring the dress that I see now seems to have sequins of some sort sewn into it. It catches the light, flicking flashes of silver around her, like a personal stellar universe. The radiance lights her face as she reaches for her cup and her skin exaggerates the colour of her large blue eyes. Holding the steaming tea in front of her, she stares down at it as though deep in thought. The jiggling of her legs sends ripples through the wooden floor and to the soles of my feet.

'It's nice to meet you. Have you come far?' I say.

'Further than I ever thought I would,' Bella replies.

'Oh dear, no wonder you look tired. Still, at least you have made it now. Where are you staying?' says Rosie.

Bella looks startled at the question and a splash of tea slops over the edge of her cup.

'Oh no, I've only just arrived. I don't know this place. I haven't organised anything yet, but as you found me outside and invited me in I thought I would take the opportunity to rest after my flight.'

'Oh, flight? You've come from overseas then?'

My nosiness begins to feel intrusive as Bella ignores the question, bending her head to wipe at the splashed tea with her hand.

'Oh don't worry about that, love,' says Rosie. 'Living with teenagers means a lot worse than a drop of tea gets spilt on that table.'

She grins but Bella does not respond as a flush of delicate pink creeps over her shadowed face.

As Rosie scrapes her chair back and bustles over to the sink to fetch a cloth she exclaims, 'Oh no, I've got to go and collect Betty from camogie training. I'm always late. She'll kill me.'

Taking this as a cue to leave, Bella and I stand up. Bella's chair crashes to the floor and I see her pale pink cheeks flush crimson as she turns to right it.

'Oh no, don't go. I fancy a good natter. I'll be back in a jiffy. Do stay, eat some cake,' and with that, in a whirl of banana fumes and flour dust, Rosie is out of the door.

Bella and I look at each other, nervousness playing on our faces as we both sit down again and focus on our tea, until I can bear the silence no longer.

'Rosie is so kind, isn't she? She's been a great friend to me.'

'Yes, I can tell she is kind, there is an aura about her,' replies Bella.

I sip from my cup and watch Bella's long thin fingers weaving in and out of each other. With more assertion than I intend I say, 'So, who is it you are looking for?'

Bella's face drains of the little colour it had so that her translucence turns to a matte white. In her widening eyes I see the glint of tears. She sits upright and after a brief pause stutters, 'Oh, oh, no one. Well, just a relative. Someone I haven't seen for years. A lifetime really.'

'What's their name? I might know them,' I say, trying to sound friendly but feeling like I am just being nosey.

'You won't know him,' Bella says and turns in her chair to gaze out of the window, back rigid and sending out a clear message to me. I take it and follow her gaze to the luxuriant and endless green vista outside the window.

'I love the hills,' she says after a while. 'They make me feel safe.'

'Me too!'

I am relieved we have found common ground, and as we both look at the green and brown mini-mountains that loom over Rosie's house I relax, listening to the clicks and creaks of the warming Aga emitting its blanket of heat.

Thinking before I speak this time, I say in a low voice, 'I do love them, and I do feel that they protect me, but you know sometimes I am scared of them too.'

Bella turns from the window to look at me across the table.

'You should be. It is right to be scared of them. They have the power to promote life in their vegetation and with their running streams, but when they are mistreated they can take away life too.'

Declan O'Brien's tragic death flashes into my mind with the memory of the men discussing destroying the hill at the centre of the site to make room for houses. My hands are trembling as I reason with myself that Bella could not have known about this event. Before I can question her further about what she means the door flings open and Rosie bustles in with both a whirlwind of energy and a sulky teenager behind her. The teenager takes one look at the three women taking over her kitchen and walks back out. Rosie looks at me and rolls her eyes.

'Phew, just made it. The caretaker was locking the gates to the pitch when I arrived. You should have seen the looks I got from madame. She wouldn't say a word to me all the way back. Thank goodness. So now, what have I missed? Did you tell Bella about the calf that escaped and ran down the road to the GAA pitch last week?' she laughed. 'Oh my, the sight of Jimmy Callaghan chasing it, oilskins flapping as much as the wisps of hair on his head will never leave me. And then when old Mrs Cronin started yelling at him to stop chasing the poor wee thing and started running down the road after him…'

Rosie's loud, infectious laugh rolled around the room as she wipes tears from her face, streaking the remnants of the flour with brown dirt. I cannot help but laugh along, even though I know this story. Catching sight of Bella looking from one to the other of us only raises the intensity of the humour and before long, Rosie and I are competing to tell of the most humorous events from the locale.

Bella is the sort of person who with her delicate frame and quiet voice makes me feel huge and clumsy, but as she relaxes with us I realise her formal manner and short answers are out of nervousness rather than the abruptness with which they are conveyed. I can see that she is very tired, her eyes sometimes half-closing and her speech slow, but also that she seems confused. I can understand that she is a stranger in town and has never been here before but the way she strains to follow our anecdotes, to understand why we are laughing, makes me feel protective towards her. I notice that she isn't drinking her tea and ask if she would like something else instead. Her eyes widen and her head leans towards me as she requests a glass of water, which she tips down her throat in a manner that somehow is dainty instead of gulping, as mine would have been.

Half an hour later, just as we were getting onto the latest scandal, Bella scrapes back her chair and announces that she has to go. Rather surprised at the abruptness of her departure Rosie and I wish her well, with Rosie reminding her to feel free to drop in anytime. With a sort of half-curtsy Bella trips out of the kitchen and we hear the front door closing with a quiet click.

Alone with a few sparkles left behind in the dusty air, Rosie and I look at each other, knowing that we are both dying to talk about this newcomer. As we tittle-tattle about how Rosie had found her on the street looking lost and cold and had invited her in, feeling sorry for her, she asks me if I had found out who she was looking for. I tell her how I had been silenced by Bella's sudden response to my queries. We shrug our shoulders and move onto the important matter of teenage girls announcing they are on some sort of new-fangled diet just as Rosie is putting dinner on the table. The rest of the afternoon passes as I had wished it, with no reference to the torpedo that Max has launched into my life.

#

I keep myself busy to distract my mind from my estrangement from Max. As I wake every morning in the still peace of the house, take my swim, stroll around the land, before cosseting myself in my studio I feel even more love for my house than ever before. It holds me and contains me, offers me a retreat and a sanctuary from the world outside. There is no way I am going to give it up, even if it means relinquishing my son to hold onto it.

The guilt though is ever-present. No matter how much I tell myself that he is grasping and uncaring, that voice of motherhood whispers in my head; perhaps if I explain to him how important the house is to me, perhaps he has reconsidered, perhaps he understands now and is longing to talk to me. I find myself jumping at sounds, thinking, hoping, dreading they may be Max coming to apologise. I come across a discarded shoe of his, long abandoned behind a chair and feel a pang of loss. When the fifth anniversary of Conor's death looms I torture myself about whether I should contact Max. As the anger at him for daring to suggest taking my house from me converts into fear that he will find a way to do so, I tell myself that it is up to him to contact me. Yet I find other reasons to relive the torture; maybe I should let him know he has left a coat here, that there is a sale on duvets coming up in town, that I have some leftover beer that I am never going to drink which he can have. Each time though I reach the same decision, a decision based on knowing that the Max I want is the one who does not exist, would not care about any of these things, who is a threat to me and my house now, and would be an unwelcome part of my life.

My nights have become sleepless again. I dream of opening the front door and finding a cat on the doorstep, thin and mangy, mewing to be let in. I slam the door on it, waking myself and taking a minute to realise it is a dream and the house is as silent at night as it is during the day. Then I stay awake for the rest of the night berating myself for having been such a failure as a mother. A mother who has raised such a callous child and who has now lost him.

#

The tiredness takes its toll and soon Rosie notices.

'You have lost the spring in your step, girl,' she says to me as we trudge up the sloping track that leads us to a view worth the effort when we make it.

'You used to do this hill in half the time, and with more interesting conversation. I'm the speedy one now. What's going on?'

The newer, trimmer Rosie slows her pace and stops to deliver a caring but determined stare at me.

'You've not been yourself for weeks, Marianne. I know you don't like to talk about personal stuff but this seems serious. I know something is not right. Can't you tell me?'

I try to walk on past her but she moves in sync with me, keeping one step in front so that I can't get past. I feel the tears brimming and am disappointed in myself. I don't want the wonderful Rosie, for whom being a mother has come so easily, to know that I am so flawed that I am estranged from my only son, the only family I have. Nor for her to know the reason why, to know how mercenary a man he has become. I am relieved when the rain that has been threatening for the last ten minutes wins its battles with the clouds, and I hold my face up to the cooling droplets, eyes closed and breathing deep into my being. As I welcome the spatters on my skin, the sensation is enhanced by the gentle embrace of Rosie's arms as she encircles me within them.

The two of us stand there and I listen to the dripping of leaves quenching their thirst. I try to tell myself that nothing else matters, that wherever I live I have what I need, and I try to believe it. I cannot let go of the image of the house I love so much, the house that means my life past and present to me, the only place I can call my own home in all of my life. The place where my love for Conor was embodied. The tension grips me as I wrestle with the urge to collapse into Rosie until, with a deep breath that turns into a snort through my nose, I step out of the embrace.

Eyes cast down to the pot-holed track as we walk, I tell her everything; that my son wants to build on the land that I love, wants to destroy it and displace me into an apartment that will be one of five in the house. I can't hold back. I tell her of the argument with Max, how I banished him from the house. I recount his childhood of brooding silences, threatening tantrums, aggressive attacks. Of his withdrawal to his room, of his refusal to acknowledge Conor as his dad, of his rejection of me as his mother. I tell how for years I have felt like nothing more than his maid, cook, and chauffer, that he had taken half of my weekly earnings from the market during the years that he lived with me, and that since he moved out he only contacts me when he wants something.

By the time I finish venting my anger and despair, the two of us are sitting in deep spongy grass at the side of the track, supported by sturdy fuchsia bushes at our backs, staring across the green rivers of fields that run down to the cliff edge. I have become expert at withholding details of my life from her over the past years. The fear of her shock and horror, her disbelief of how bad my relationship with Max is has a hold over me. It is stronger than the rational voice that tries to soothe me, to reassure me that Rosie is accepting and uncritical.

When the words dry up, I look at her. Her face too is streaked with tears, and she swipes at her nose in a rough manner before reaching for my hand. With the two of us sitting in the ditch like a pair of confused leprechauns her husky voice gathers volume as she speaks

'Well first of all, of course he shouldn't have asked you. What a cheek. In fact, how unfeeling altogether, if you don't mind me saying so, love.'

I hide my shudder of embarrassment with a small smile.

'I know what that house means to you. It's not the same I know, but even for me, living in the house I grew up in, and my mother grew up in before me, means that I feel a love for it and its history. I would rather die than give it up.'

I feel a twinge of disappointment at these words of Rosie's. It is not the same. My house does not have a history of generations of Fairmans. My house was supposed to be the start of our history, not the end. To let it go would be the letting go of the only dream I have had since childhood. Perhaps I should not have said so much. As I had always anticipated, I cannot expect anyone else to understand.

'For you though, it's about Conor and having a family isn't it?'

Rosie has read my mind. She does understand. I nod through tears and a running nose.

'You are completely right not to give it up but you are completely wrong to blame for yourself for what he is doing. We each of us just do our best as mothers, and there comes a time when the little darlings must make their own choices. If those choices are wrong it is not our fault. Guilt will eat you up, love, and then what do you have? A half-eaten bag of nerves.'

I gaze into her caring brown eyes. Of course she is right. With her sensitive insightfulness she has cut through my despair, and we both smile through our tears at her stupid joke. I hope the gratitude I feel leaps from my heart to hers.

After another hour we agree that we are now starting to feel the chill rising from the damp grass, Rosie and I ease ourselves up to get walking again, with lots of groans and grabs at our lower backs. As we descend towards the unsettled murky grey sea I say, 'What am I going to do, Rosie? I don't want to lose the house, but I don't want to lose Max forever either. He's the only family I have, and I'm all he has, whether he cares or not. I don't know what will become of him if I abandon him. But it's so hard. I am so ashamed of him, and of me for having raised him to be the man he is. Sometimes I feel I can hardly look at him but. I still can't let him go completely.'

'You know what, my girl, I think you carry on doing just what you are doing. Stay busy and leave him to stew a bit. He'll come round. He won't want to lose you either when he really thinks about it. Give him time.'

I don't have Rosie's confidence in believing that Max will return to me but now, as the clouds part to let the sunshine back, and feeling infused with Rosie's love and understanding, I am happy to believe her. I know Rosie will help me to stay strong in my resolve. As we walk back to the gates of the house where we will separate, I plan my next quilt. This one will be made from the remnants of grey towels with splashes of bright yellow.

#

Today the morning is bright, and I am pleased to be setting out for the market. The new quilt, on top of a pile of others, visible in my rear-view mirror as I drive to town, reminds me that Rosie's advice has helped. I have kept myself occupied and resisted urges to contact Max. I haven't heard from him, but with every day that passes I feel stronger and more determined to hold my position.

Rosie is there when I arrive at the market, setting up her stall and chatting to Bella, who as usual is quiet but attentive, reminding me of myself when I first arrived there. We have got used to Bella now. She started turning up at the market from the first Saturday after she had arrived in town. Looking lost and a little confused in the melee of people, stalls, and music of the market on a sunny day, we beckoned her over. She stayed the rest of the morning with us, joining in with the laughter but not saying very much. Over the past six Saturdays though she has become as much of a fixture as Rosie and I are. Rosie brings an extra fold-up chair with her and the three of us while away the mornings by our stalls, chatting to each other and the other stallholders and customers. Bella's formal mannerisms are still discernible but she is more relaxed with us now, offering to get our coffees, and greeting people as they come and go.

Seeing me arrive, Rosie chirrups, 'Good, you're here. Let's get the coffees.'

With a smile she turns to Bella and says, 'Sorry, two coffees and a hot milk.'

It has become a joke between the three of us that Bella does not drink tea or coffee, preferring only milk or water. We had accused her of depriving herself in order to stay so thin, but she has convinced us that she just doesn't like these beverages that keep us going from morning to night. At least she joins us in eating cake, taking tiny nibbles that are in stark contrast to the mouthfuls that Rosie and I cram in.

I love the way that Bella dresses. With no apparent self-consciousness she wears eye-catching flowing clothes, always printed with flowers or animals, usually butterflies, that swish and float around her and accentuate her tiny figure. A straw bonnet, bedecked with real flowers, sets off the outfits. No need for any make-up, her skin always glows, and her large blue eyes are bright and gleaming with curiosity. She is the picture of health with an ethereal quality that allows her to blend into the background or appear as if from nowhere in front of us. She is a child-woman who seems innocent of the ways of the world yet keen to find them out. Rosie and I have taken her to our hearts, although still know little about where she has come from or why she is here.

As Bella helps me lay out my quilts she admires them, stroking the coloured squares, and identifying each embroidered flower. When I show her a quilt embroidered with butterflies she claps her hands so gently that no sound emanates, and springs up and down like a ballerina with wings. She loves nature and knows all the names of plants, flowers and herbs. She educates Rosie and I on their uses so that we start looking for medicinal and edible flora on our walks.

Today is bright and warm and the mood in the market is of relaxed wandering. Customers are keen to stay and chat as they browse the stalls and I make many sales. It is as though, lifted by the sunlight, people don't care about money today. To my delight I sell three quilts at one hundred euros each in addition to receiving three commissions, one for an 'anniversary quilt' tailored to the colours requested by a young couple, another as a winter warmer, and the third as a surprise gift from a husband for his wife. I also receive two visits from the bearded barista who I now know is called Aiden and is single. When two o'clock comes and the market starts emptying, I feel full of energy and reluctant for the day to end.

'Hey, how about we go back to my house and drink iced tea in the garden?' I say to Rosie and Bella.

It is unusual for me to entertain at the house. I much prefer the inviting cosiness of Rosie's kitchen for chats than the decaying vastness of my house. Max and I never had visitors, and I have done little to make it welcoming to anyone other than myself. It is still only partially restored. The rooms that I use are cosy but shabby. Much of the house is inhabited only by mice and wild cats. Rosie knows the kitchen and my sitting-room and has always been curious to see the rest of the house, but my embarrassment at its state has stopped me showing it to her. Today though, the weather is so glorious that we can sit in the garden. Nature takes care of that all year round so that it is always beautiful.

'Oh yes, let's,' says Rosie. 'I love your place. It's a beautiful old house, Bella, with amazing gardens. It will be gorgeous to sit out there this afternoon.'

With that decided, we start packing away our stalls. I leave before them with a farewell toot of the car horn, knowing that Rosie will be embroiled in chat with other market stallholders for a while yet. I want to get back to prepare, in time to prevent Rosie and Bella needing to enter the house. I should have known my efforts would be futile.

'Cooee, we're here.' I hear Rosie's trill as I am walking up the stairs from the kitchen. I try to hasten my pace without losing the glasses, jug of iced tea or market-bought cake from the tray I am balancing. I want to halt her at the front door and usher her back out to the garden but my caution is my failure and from the hallway I hear, 'Your house is soooo amazing, Marianne.' As I approach her, she whispers 'You must never let that boy get his hands on it.'

Stuck with the tray and nowhere to put it down I am powerless to stop Rosie wandering through the hallway towards the drawing room.

'Wow, what a lot of books. I knew you were a reader but not quite how much of one. Have you read all of these?'

'Oh they're not all mine,' I reply.

This is ridiculous, I am getting hot and agitated in my search for a nearby surface to put the tray down on so that I can chase Rosie out of the house and away from the possibility of her seeing Max's scribblings or the hateful graffiti he left on the walls when he was angry with me.

'What?' Rose's voice is distant as she ventures further into the room.

'Lots of them belong to Max,' I shout, at last putting the tray down on the bench by the front door and hastening across the hallway.

'Come on, let's go outside. It's gorgeous out there, Let's make the most of it.'

Anxiety sloshes about in my stomach. I don't want anyone, not even Rosie, looking into my life like this. I feel exposed and shaky.

'Hellllooooo,' Rosie has come back into the hall and, head back, is calling up into the high ceiling vaults. 'It's vast Marianne. You could fit ten families in this hall alone. All this space. It's gorgeous. I'd love to see the views from upstairs…' She lowers her head and looks at me questioningly. I pretend I haven't noticed.

'Come on, Rosie, Please can we go outside. I want more of that sunshine. Besides, we've left Bella all alone out there.'

'Oh I'm sure she's ok. I think she has started her own tour of the gardens.' Rosie laughs, and then with a tinge of regret in her voice as she picks up on my anxiety, 'Come on then, I guess we had better go and find her. Here give me those glasses. I'll help you carry.'

I scan the gardens as we approach the lawn.

'Bella,' calls Rosie, 'Come on, iced tea is ready.'

Bella's tiny form emerges from the woods, and she trips over to us as we flap a blanket onto the fresh dry grass and arrange ourselves on it. Rosie and I sprawl but Bella sits upright, tucking her tiny feet under her.

'Isn't this just heavenly?' chirrups Rosie, slurping iced tea as she reaches for a large slice of cake.

'We can swim in the lake later if you like, I do almost every morning,' I boast.

Rosie looks slightly alarmed at my suggestion, but Bella looks horrified. I withdraw it.

'It's ok, we don't have to, just an idea.'

'I think we are both quite happy staying right here,' says Rosie, diffusing the atmosphere so that a calmness descends as we are all soothed by the sun's warmth. I rest my eyes on the still views of distant fields dotted with black and white cows illuminated in the lake's shimmer.

Restless as usual, it is not long before Rosie breaks the silence.

'Come on Bella, I bet you haven't seen anything as beautiful as this before?'

We have to lean towards her to hear Bella's reply.

'It's beautiful' she whispers, 'It reminds me of where I came from.'

'Don't tell me you live in a place like this too. Am I the only one who lives in a two-up two-down ordinary house?' says Rosie.

'Oh no, my house is quite different,' replies Bella.

A shadow crosses her face, and she looks down. Catching Rosie's eye I see that she can't resist the tease.

'Oh yes? What's it like?'

It works. Rosie's enquiry prompts an outpouring from Bella about the beauty of where she lives. Her house is only one storey and that is fine because she lives alone and anyway spends as much time as she can outdoors. Her job is something to do with preserving nature and she is responsible for a team of workers who cover a wide area made up of a mixture of meadows, fields, and scrubland. It sounds like she is some sort of ranger, who lives in a lodge house in a country park. We want to know more; where this place is, why she is here, but although the picture of her home comes to life with Bella's words, Rosie and I are no closer to knowing why she has left it to come here on a search, or who she is looking for.

Today though it doesn't seem important. As we settle into chat and peaceful silences, I feel the remnants of the tension I have been carrying ebbing away into the summer air. After wearing it for so long I am relaxed, my body pressing into the cushioning grass, my mind floating with the directionless conversation.

As the afternoon sun heads over the house behind us, I feel sleepy, until Bella rouses me with a suggestion that we all take a walk around the woods. Rosie and I make half-hearted attempts to stay where we are but our protests are in vain. Leaving the remnants of the cake and dregs of iced tea where they are, we drag ourselves upright and wander towards the woods.

As we cross the expanse of lawn, I try to deflect the stabs of sadness starting to attack at the thought of losing this place enters my mind again. When Rosie suggests we take our shoes off to feel the changing of the ground from grassy softness to prickling woodiness Bella becomes so excited she seems to bounce along as we walk. Wandering barefoot through the pine scented woodland in light that changes from golden to caramel as we pass between trees helps to push aside the thoughts, but I am quiet and pensive.

By the time we emerge, Rosie has her usual panic about needing to collect a child from a games pitch and sits down on the blanket to squeeze her tatty trainers over her bare feet. Bella springs up too, muttering that she must go. As the departure of my friends allows the shroud of my despondency to drop over me, I congratulate myself that I succeeded in keeping Max's toxicity from infecting my friends. I watch them leave, and take another look over my land, breathing fresh air in and love for it out.

#

It has now been two months since my argument with Max. I have softened towards him but not towards his proposal. My life now is tranquil but uneasy. Max is on my mind more and I hear snippets of information about him from the market traders and customers. He seems to be out and about in town again now, presumably scouting for land and hoping that the resentment towards him for his lack of concern about Donal's accident is receding, but is often seen drunk, lurching from pub to pub with a group of rowdy friends. He does not seem to be doing much to garner any more respect than he ever has from the townspeople, and he has not won any from me either.

Not knowing how Max is coping with my rejection of him, and fearing his revenge, disrupts me in strange ways. I think I hear noises day and night, and rush to the window to see if it is him coming up the driveway. I see fleeting figures, disappearing into long unused rooms, or dashing between trees, and imagine it is him sneaking into the house. Settling myself afterwards is trying, and even with my work to focus on, my concentration wanders. I can manage the days, but the nights are beset with dreams and maybe-dreams that invade and bother me so that I am relieved to see the first rays of dawn when they come.

Tonight though, the dawn seems as far away as my life with Great Aunt Alice is. I had worked on the final squares of a quilt that captured the daily changing seasons of the weather, interspersing sunburst yellow with black thunderous, and blue-grey squares, in the hope that I would tire myself into uninterrupted sleep. I did fall asleep straight after going to bed but awoke a couple of hours later from a dream about encountering a car crash as I walked along the high street of the tiny village I had lived in as a child. As I got closer, I could make out the driver slumped over the steering wheel, covered in blood and clearly dead. As I ran to the car it seemed to move further away but I could see that the body was Max. Calling out to him, I saw him open one bloodied eye and wink at me. Waking with a jolt, tears streaming down my face, I am disorientated for a minute. I struggle to remind myself that Max is not dead, but is lost to me.

In that limbo between sleep and full wakefulness, waves of sadness engulf me. I let the tears flow until my eyes are dry and stinging, and I have none left. Feeling for my slippers on the cold wooden floor I catch a glimpse of light in the woods and pulling back the thin curtains, I peer out into the mist-filled darkness. The sky and land are merged into one canvas of black. No stars light the sky and the moon has deserted us tonight. I hear the swoop of an owl but cannot see it. There is nothing else moving out there and I am about to turn away when I see the flicker of an orange streak amongst the trees. I know that this time I have not imagined it and am compelled to go and investigate.

Five minutes later I am stepping out into the cool, dark silence. I feel like the only person on earth and the feeling gives me a brave determination. I walk across the lawn towards just discernible silhouettes of trees, now seeing the orange flickers larger and more frequently. It looks like a fire and I feel palpitations in my throat. As my pace increases I tell with myself that there is no reason for there to be a fire in the woods. Until today's burst of sunshine, the weather has been its usual damp self and the grey mist I am striding through an almost permanent feature of both day and night. Yet if it is not a fire I cannot imagine what would be throwing out these flares.

There is a dense stillness, wetter and darker than the one on the lawn, and scented with odours that err on just the right side of unpleasant. The silence sizzles with faint skitterings of animals and hissing of trees and plants absorbing moisture. Reaching the woods I feel the ground change beneath my feet, as I had done earlier in the day with Rosie and Bella. I am wearing wellingtons but still the springy hardness of the grass turning to crunchy woodland notifies the sensitive soles of my feet. It does little to distract me as I peer ahead, looking for the next orange streak. I can smell fire now, smoky and woody, a crackle shoots out orange sparks and spurts of acid shoot fear into my stomach. Can the woods really be on fire?

With no warning I see it in a small clearing, a small campfire, popping as it devours its fuel, throwing up small fireworks of orange that momentarily blind me. My first thought is of Max. Is he conjuring up revenge by trying to burn the land? I hasten towards the fire, stumbling over tree roots and pushing branches away as they reach for my face. Entering the clearing I feel the change of air as space opens up around me. I see a figure lying down, too small to be Max, childlike and still. I am tiptoeing now, heart beating fast. I peer over the fire and down at the sleeping form. It is Bella.

I feel the heat seeping into my legs but the fire's warmth does not help the freeze in my brain. Bella is asleep by a fire in the woods on my land. Maybe I did not wake up, have somehow walked into the flames of the car wreck, have slipped into another dreamscape. Sense, of a sort, begins to come when Bella opens her eyes and leaps up, scattering leaves from her dress as she does so.

'Marianne.'

She is as bereft of words as I am.

'What's going on, Bella? What are you doing here?' is all I can stutter.

'I'm sorry, Marianne, I'm sorry. I am living here.'

We look at each other, she with her head cocked to one side, me with creased forehead staring, trying to make sense of this. She helps me out.

'When we came here the other day I felt drawn to the woods. They feel like home. I cannot resist their beauty and peacefulness, and they give me what I need to survive. I have no money. I had been sleeping in the alleyways in town until now but when I saw these woods I knew they were perfect. I have been coming at night. Look, I started building a shelter over there.'

She points to a humped shape near the boggy stream that feeds the lake.

'I have been working when its dark and gathering materials during the days. I can get water from the stream, and I eat the berries and fruit from the trees. I'm sorry but once or twice I have taken some of your vegetables from your garden. I'm so sorry Marianne, I should have told you.'

At this moment I feel only relief. This explains the noises I have been hearing, the flitting figure I have been seeing in my garden. I thought I was going mad with worry about Max, imagining fairies, or worse, intruders, but it has been Bella who I have spotted in the shadows, heard rustling in the garden. Drained, I slide down against a tree trunk to take this in. Bella looks at me with concern.

'Are you angry, Marianne? I can leave, find somewhere else.'

'No,' I say with some hesitation. 'No, I am not angry. You need to live somewhere.'

As I say the words an idea begins to unfold in my head.

'Come and stay in the house. It's huge and empty, I am there on my own. We won't get in each other's way.'

As the words create the image in my head, the notion becomes perfect. Bella will breathe new energy into the house. She will introduce a freshness to its stale air, be company for me, inspire me to take better care of the house, and of myself.

Now I am the one with the beseeching look. It is so obvious to me that this is the best thing to do, it will help Bella and it will help me. The house can be lived in again, really lived in. Bella's answer surprises me, and I swallow my disappointment.

'Thank you but no, Marianne, I have space here and all that I need. I can think and am managing just fine. It reminds me of my home. I love being outdoors.'

So, she doesn't want to live with me, nor to move indoors. I am surprised to feel a little envious at her certainty. I know so little about this woman, appearing out of the blue, searching for someone unknown, choosing to live outdoors, but I can see her complete oneness with nature and her outdoor life. Trying not to show my disappointment I tell her I understand and am happy she has found a home on my land.

She smiles, 'Thank you, Marianne, that means a lot to me. Would you like to see the house that I am building?'

Of course I would. Bella leads me the short distance to the half-built shelter she has been constructing. Twigs and leaves are woven into a sturdy curved structure, sealed at the ground by compressed mud that creates a dry floor. At the back there is a pile of fresh leaves, presumably her bed, and on one side a couple of dresses are draped over a supporting branch. From the hut roof hang bunches of drying herbs that scent the air. The shimmer from the dresses seems to amplify the light that is coming through the woven roof as dawn approaches. It flecks the floor with sparkles. The hut feels cosy and I want to cocoon myself in the leaf bed and breathe in the woody scent, but Bella ushers me back out to the fire which she has banked up and has a pot of water suspended from a stand made of branches over it.

'I can make rosehip tea. Would you like that?' she smiles, assuming my affirmative answer and indicates the blanket she had been sleeping on. I sit down under the natural canopy of a giant weeping willow and watch her small, thin pale fingers picking rosehips from a nearby bush. Listening to the birds starting to wake up and call to each other across the wood I could stay here forever.

We sit cross-legged on either side of the fire, sipping from tiny cups made of hollowed out wood. Bella is relaxed now that she knows I am happy for her to stay. In this environment she exudes a confidence that I have not seen in her anywhere else. Her petite form, wrapped in a cape adorned with real flowers, blends in with the undergrowth, and she begins to talk, more so than I have ever known her to. She tells me that she has always been uncomfortable around people, feeling different and out of place, until she met Rosie and me. She has lived happily with nature for most of her life, staying away from people and caring for plants and animals. Her eyes have a faraway look, and I can see her mind is back at her home. It feels invasive to interrupt and her soft voice has a soothing lilt that I am content to sit and listen to.

On our third cup she turns the conversation to me, catching me unawares.

'What about you Marianne, who are you? Tell me about your life.'

From this tiny person comes this huge question. The question I have been asking myself since I lost Conor, and realised that I was no mother to Max. I don't know who I am or what my life is. When I think back on it, as I am prompted to do by her question, I see only tragedy; the loss of my mother, my austere upbringing with Great Aunt Alice, my fleeting flirtation with happiness when I met Conor, the sorrow of losing him whilst gaining Max, the challenges of raising Max only to lose him now, the dashing of my hopes when Conor returned a broken man, and the final tragedy of his suicide. How can I answer Bella?

Her expectant face looks at me through the lightening gloom and I decide I am going to tell her about the Conor I fell in love with. It feels right somehow to talk of love in this glade of serenity. I tell her of his charm and wittiness, of his intellect and enthusiasm for life, of our instant connection when we first met. I spoke about how he understood my shyness and wasn't put off by it, about our shared love of nature and wild swimming. How we used to escape the city as often as we could to go on aimless rambles around the countryside, discovering hidden beaches and deserted headlands. I recalled for her the day we stumbled across the house during one of these afternoons and both saw its rows of windows as welcoming eyes, and its half-open front door as an invitation to enter. I even tell her how we swam naked in the lake that day and then made love in one of the bedrooms on the dusty floor. I tell Bella what a special man Conor was and about how much he wanted to restore the house into a family home and fill it with our children. How much he would have enjoyed being a father.

After saying so much to Bella about this man she had never met, I hesitate to continue. The sun is burning off the mist now and I can see her face, curious and intent. I know the sad ending to this fairy tale and looking at Bella's shining eyes I do not want to bring down onto her the despair that followed our romance. I do not want to speak of the confusion I felt when he disappeared, of the challenge of holding firm to the belief that he would not have chosen to leave me despite everyone gossiping about what sort of woman I must have been, about the difficulties I had over the years with Max as an unpopular child who bullied other children until none wanted to be friends with him. How I felt that the town shunned us, leaving him alone with me. I do not want to confess my heartbreak about failing to create the home that Conor wanted or my failure to have been the mother for his son that he would have wished for. I do not want to hear myself speaking of admitting defeat in being able to care for Conor when he returned and of how it nearly broke me to agree to admit him to psychiatric care. I cannot speak of his death. So instead, I keep the fairy tale going by telling her how much I loved him and still believe that he is with me, loving me back. How our love is the foundation of the house, regardless of its physical state, and that I can never live anywhere else, and so do understand why she wants to live on its land.

My voice now is husky with emotion. I can feel tears threatening as I tell her then of how our love was taken from us in events that still do not make sense. I feel release. I can see Conor's face as I sob and with Bella looking on I feel comforted. It as though if I keep talking about him I have him back. Joy flecked with piercing sadness subsumes my body.

I am surprised to see that Bella too is crying. Her tears, delicate and transparent, drip into her lap and the familiar burn of guilt overtakes me as the images of Conor disperse.

'It's ok, Bella, it was a long time ago. I am a different person now. I have my market stall, and Rosie. And the house of course.'

Clearing my throat, I continue, 'You would have liked Conor. He loved nature too. He was teaching himself to whittle wood before he disappeared and was clearing a copse here in the woods. He loved this place. He thought it was magical. You see that hawthorn tree over there? He said we could never cut it because it was a fairy tree and to harm it would bring bad luck.'

We lapse into silence as I contemplate that the bad luck came anyway. The fire is crackling its final sparks and I start to feel the chill of the dampness of the earth seeping through the blanket. I push myself up, flicking my hair away from my face and shaking my head to sniff away my grief.

'I must go. Are you sure you are alright here? Do you want to come in for breakfast?'

I don't want her to. I want to be alone. To try and bring Conor back into my head again in the safety of the house. Her gentle declining of my invitation belies my anxiety and I make a brusque farewell to leave the woods as fast as I can. The heat of the daylight out on the lawn again contrasts with the dazed and darkened entry to the woods last night and brings me back to this life again. I see the house in front of me as my legs tread the familiar path back to my bed.

Chapter 10

I slept through all of yesterday and fitfully last night, but waking up this morning I feel refreshed and energised, lightened and liberated by my outpouring to Bella. I feel calm and free. I am a single woman with responsibility only to myself. My swim today is luxurious, my body in perfect harmony with the water's ripples and splashes. I am a mermaid, at home in this soothing environment, cutting through the water, diving down to its silence.

Back on land my human feet have a new bounce in them as I head back to the house planning on a coffee, banana and fresh egg boiled for exactly three minutes. Then I will sit by an open window and finish the quilt I started yesterday.

In the kitchen I turn on the radio and hum along to the classics of my youth. Pottering about with the kettle, the egg waiting to be boiled beside it. I lean on the bar of the Aga, warming my backside.

The knock at the door is so quiet that at first I think I have imagined it and resume my singalong. When the song ends I hear it again and I go to answer, sure that it will be Bella.

'You don't have to knock… oh.'

It's not Bella standing on my doorstep, it's Max. Butterflies flit around in my stomach and blood rushes through my ears drowning the tranquillity that had been establishing itself there.

'Hi Ma.'

Max's smile doesn't reach those eyes of Conor's on his face, and although his body tilts towards me, almost as if he wants to embrace me, I know better and stand unmoving in the doorway.

'Ma, I had to come and see you. If I say I'm sorry can I come in?'

He only ever calls me Ma when he wants something. Hearing him use it puts me on my guard but still a flicker of hope ignites inside me. Maybe it is reconciliation that he wants today.

'Max, come in, let's talk. Kettle's just boiled. Come down to the kitchen.'

I hold the door beckoning him in and a Cheshire Cat grin spreads across his face as he hops over the threshold. Already I wonder if I have given in too easily, been sucked in at the first challenge. He is my son though, he is Conor's child. Conor, who I saw only last night, would want us to reunite.

In the kitchen, I busy myself emptying the full kettle and refilling it, asking Max with my back turned whether he has eaten, or would like me to boil him an egg. I hear no sound from him but his presence seeps into me like an encircling coil, gripping me so my breathing becomes uneven. As I bustle I hold one hand to my chest.

When I have run out of things to do, I turn to him, cup of tea in hand, its contents slopping a little over the side. I put it down on the table in front of him with a louder thump than I had intended and sit in the chair opposite. I look at him.

My son is now a man. His handsome face looks more worn than when I last saw him, and he has cut his hair, but he is clean-shaven, and wearing a neat navy jumper over pressed jeans. His figure is bulkier than it has been, maybe from the drinking? Max is the same age that Conor and I were when we met. I study his eyes to see if Conor is beneath them. Although more deep set, Max's eyes still flash emerald green like Conor's did and when he flicks his hair off his face, I am taken right back to Conor. I give myself a small shake. This is Max and not Conor, and Max must be here for a reason. I hope it's the same reason that I want it to be.

Max stares down at his fingers intertwined on the table. Not one part of his body or his face moves. Something emanates from him that I cannot make sense of. There is the usual menace, but it is softened by something new, something indecipherable. I am determined not to be cowed by him, to hold my ground, not to be seduced into handing over the house. I place my hands on the table in an opposite gesture to his; apart, palms flat. I want him to see that I am resolute but open to him.

'Ma. Mum, I don't know what I was thinking. I am sorry. I hope you can forgive me. I know how much you love this house and I would never do anything to take it away from you.'

This is unexpected. I want to welcome it, to believe the words, to trust the sentiment behind them, but my heart resists. For too long I have known not to trust my son.

'Max, threatening me and the house like you did was probably the most upsetting thing you have ever done.'

'I know, Mum, I know, and I am so sorry.'

Is he?

'But it wasn't all my fault.'

And there it is. The Max who takes no blame, puts responsibility for his actions on others. I sit up in the chair as he continues.

'I was so keen to be promoted at work that I didn't think about your feelings. I was thoughtless.'

Tingles dance their way down my spine to the pit of my stomach. He wants something.

'I should treat you better. I know I should. It was a terrible thing to suggest. Can we just forget about it? I have something much more exciting to tell you.'

I feel trepidation. Am I being manipulated?

'Mum, I'm getting married.'

He puts his face in one hand and folds his lips inwards with a triumphant smirk. He thinks he has me. Expectation spreads across his face. A smile sits at his mouth, but his eyes give him away. They are flat, no depth, no feeling.

'You're getting married?' I stutter.

I have never seen him with a woman. He has never talked about girlfriends, and as far as I have heard, all his socialising is with local lads, down at the pubs in town. My fingers curl a little, fingernails scraping the table.

'Yes Mum, I have found the girl, the woman,' he corrects himself, 'the woman I want to spend the rest of my life with.'

It sounds too rehearsed. My trepidation puts my body on full alert, stiff and rigid on the outside, liquid and swirling inside. There is something not right about this. I cannot believe that Max is ready to change his life by getting married. His priorities have always been about himself, not about caring for others.

'Tell me more, Max. Who is she, how did you meet? When can I meet her?'

His eyes widen. He is not prepared for this, thought that I would take him at his word without question. In the flash of anger I see in his eyes, I can tell without doubt that there is no woman. He is lying to me and I can hardly breathe for guessing the reason why.

I had so wanted his reappearance to be an opportunity for us to forge a new bond. A chance for me to show him love by standing firm but keeping him in my life. I slump down in the chair, stretching my legs long and wide under the table, and let my thoughts drift away as I look at Max floundering for words. Whatever he is saying is meaningless. I don't believe him and whoever, or whatever, he is describing will be lies too.

I think about Bella out there in the woods, on a quest and living a simple life. How shocked she would be to meet this man, listen to his falsehoods, recognise his mendacity, and know that he is my son. I am relieved that I spoke only about Conor to her and not about Max. I fear for what I would have unleashed in that afternoon of revelation if I allowed my true feelings about the person who Max is to be made real by speaking them out loud.

'Mother, you're not listening.'

I snap back, alerted by his change in language. I am no longer Ma but Mother again. The person he can taunt and torture, the person he thinks he can manipulate and use. This is the moment the wheedling stops and the demands begin.

'So, you see I'm going to need security, something to start married life with.'

Even to speak is hard for me, and the words fall out in a sigh,

'What do you mean, Max? What security? Do you need money?'

It is an effort to look at him, but I force myself to catch and hold his glare with what I hope is a steely look. This man, this child, this son of mine who once held so many promises of love and happiness for me, is now someone I despise. He has given me no reason to revise my determination to hold him to account for his challenge to my land. If he were not my son I would see him only as a self-centred and uncaring money-grabber who thinks that a few lies will con me into giving into him. I do not understand how he can be Conor's child. Conor was so capable of love, and of generating love. This misfit offspring is the very opposite of what he was. He is not open to being loved and has spent his life rejecting my attempts. His heart is as hard as his eyes.

I break the stare first as I feel the familiar wetness gathering behind my own eyes. He must not see me cry. I don't need to worry; he doesn't even notice. Or care.

'No. I don't want your money, Mother.'

How proud he is. I know that his life is predicated on the accumulation of money. To ask for it would be an admission of failure for this man.

'Not money, Mother, security I said. Security. I need the land. This land. I need to be able to rely on a secure income in married life.'

That's it. It's over. I don't shout or try to strike him. I don't scream or rant or tell him that I don't believe there is any woman he is going to marry. All I do is say in a hushed voice designed to subdue the quavering in it

'Max, I need you to leave now. To leave me. To go. I have told you before this land is not to be built on and I mean it. If you think that you can lie to me and manipulate your way onto it you are wrong. Just go please. Now.'

His faces flushes purple as he scrapes back his chair. Those eyes shoot out a menacing stare. He knows he is defeated, and he is angry. His hands are folded into fists, and he leans across the table to close in on me, but I am not frightened. I look directly at him again as he says, 'Fine. If you are happy to see me in the gutter then so be it. I thought that you might love me enough to help me towards happiness, Mother, but if that is beyond you then I'll just find my own way. But don't think I won't have this land. I will, you know, and then I will build on it.'

The slam of the kitchen door echoes through the house as he takes the stairs three at a time. His footsteps shake the floorboards above when he marches across the hall and out of the house. The crash of the front door is the last pillar of our relationship hurtling down into that black hole where all the other failed efforts lie. The house shivers at his departure. As it settles, I allow my tears to come, raining guilt and sorrow out of my whole body. Wracking with sobs I know that I never did love him enough. Nothing I did was enough to mask that, to warm his coldness, shake his indifference, teach him to love. Now he is an aggressive, unfeeling man whose need to satiate himself with material success knows no bounds. His poison arrows pierce everyone he encounters, bringing sorrow, anger, and yes, even death. And he has fired them at me more than at anyone else. He has failed me, and I have failed him. I lower my head onto my arms on the table and let my failure flood out of me.

#

For days after, I wallow in self-pity, berating myself for being the mother who raised a child to become a man like Max. Those who have whispered and gossiped about me for years are right. I didn't know how to raise a child. I wasn't a good enough mother.

I am rent in two in by failure. I am a woman who has lost both husband and son. A woman who was once a wife and mother is now neither. I was so meaningless to my husband that he preferred to die than to return to me. I was such a bad mother that I raised a cold, heartless bully of a man and have thrust him away. I long to start again, have a second chance. I want Conor back and I want to know why my dream of a happy family life has been denied to me.

I spend hours thinking over and over what Conor had told me about his time away, of how joyous it had been, of how it was unmatched by the world he found himself in on his return, of his despair at ever finding such a place again. If only I could understand where he went, why he went and what made him come back. So many possibilities flit through my mind, the most obvious being that he left me for another woman. It didn't make sense though – he never left the town except with me, we had both been open about our previous relationships, or in my case, lack of them, and I know, just know, that he truly loved me. Our talk of our future together, plans for the house, dreams of a family, they could not have been made in deceit. No, he must have been forced to leave, somehow lured or taken away. Who or what could have taken him, and for so long? What could have been forceful enough to draw him away?

The questions kept coming, but no answers with them. My imagination veers from the logical to the fantastical; he had an accident, lost his memory, was kidnapped, became ill. As my agony of not knowing gnawed at me over the days, my mind kept returning to the talk of fairies – how they entice people to their kingdom and show them the time of their lives, time that passes in one night there but takes seven years in our human time. I know it is nonsense of course, but in my desperation to find a hook upon which to rest my confusion it seems more and more likely.

Perhaps he had been pixie-led by a bright light that drew him to a beautiful, shining fairy castle on his way home from the pub that night? Perhaps once there he had joined in the wild dancing, entranced by the music? Perhaps he had been lured into the arms of the Fairy Queen and soothed into a blissfulness unequalled by his time in my arms? Perhaps all this has been punishment from the fairies for living in this house, built on their land? My mind draws me further and further in – perhaps he conceived a child with the Queen? Being a half-fairy, half-human child, perhaps it was exchanged for a fully human one to be taken to be raised as a servant by the fairies? My thoughts race as they veer backwards and forwards from me to Max to Conor to me to Max to motherhood to loss. Maybe the changeling child is Max? It's crazy but just for a few hours, having this explanation eases my distress.

In my tormented state it all starts to make sense. It explains why my life has been so hard. Why I lost not only my husband but also motherhood as I had dreamed it. I am being punished. All I have ever wanted is what others have – a happy marriage, a loving family, a welcoming home. If we hadn't moved to this house, if he hadn't followed the light, if I hadn't put all my hopes into one man…

#

One day, after wallowing in my own despair, hardly leaving the bed, unwashed and uncaring, I hear Rosie calling up from the hallway.

'Marianne? Marianne? Are you here, love? Is everything alright?'

I roll over, wafts of sour-smelling sweat drifting from my body, as her voice drifts up the stairs. I pull the lank duvet over my head, not ready for the world yet, not even for Rosie.

'I let myself in, love, just wanted to check you're ok. I've brought a bowl of stew for you.'

I can hear her waiting, imagine her straining her head to listen for any sound from me but I remain unmoving in my duvet-shrouded world and hope that she does not come upstairs.

'I'm going to look around the garden for you. Call up to me sometime, will you?'

I hear the thud of her feet striding back to the front door and when it closes behind her I throw off the duvet and lie on my back staring at the familiar cracks in the plaster above until I fall asleep again.

#

It is after a full week in bed that I leave it. I can hardly bear my own filthiness now. My hair feels thin and matted and hangs limply around my face, which feels oily and shiny. I have only drunk water from the bathroom tap and eaten Jacobs crackers from packets beside my bed for this past week, both appetite and energy drained by my self-pity. Today though, the crackers have run out and the bathroom tap water tastes sour. I have a craving for a cup of sweet tea. Wincing as my body creaks its way out of the bed, I reach for my tattered dressing gown, and give up on bending down to retrieve my slippers from underneath the bed. My legs feel both shaky and stiff and I move close to the wall so that I can drag a steadying hand along it as I cross the room and start along the corridor, trying not to be repelled by the smell coming from my armpits. Reaching the bottom of the staircase I feel so weak that I sit on the bottom step, head in filthy hands to take a rest before finishing my journey.

I am half asleep again before I know it so jolt my head up and reach to the stair rail to pull myself up. I notice a bowl of food next to a pile of post on the hall table, and remember Rosie's visit, two, or was it three days ago? Perhaps if I can eat the food she has left I will feel a bit stronger. It is hard crossing the hall, and I notice that the floorboards do not give their customary groans and squeaks. Have I lost that much weight?

The food of course is cold, lumps of grey meat stuck like fossils in amber in congealed fat, trapped with pale orange carrots and puke-green peas. Yet it provokes pangs of hunger and I scoop some out with my fingers, germs and filth be damned. It is repellent but after eating like a wild woman for a few minutes I feel energy begin a sluggish journey around my body. I stand a little straighter.

Spotting the curling mass of junk mail, once soggy with rain and now dried out into crumpled sheets on the table, I am about to walk away until I notice an A4 sized stiff brown envelope that seems to have been impervious to the vagaries of rain and sleet that had attacked its flimsy advertisement companions. This is something different. I pick it up.

My fingers tingle with expectation as I fumble with the firm glued opening. The letter is an official one and I wonder with mounting anxiety what it can be. With an impatience to put myself out of the frustration of not knowing I tear through the unyielding brown envelope, pulling a jagged diagonal scar across it until it rips in two. Black writing on thick white paper exposes itself as thin leaflets and a stamped addressed envelope drift to the floor. I do not even contemplate picking them up and my already shaking legs turn to unset jelly as the writing comes into focus:

'Murphy, O'Shea, and Finn
Solicitors
Legacies and Ownership Department
Grassville
Co. Kerry'

The effort of remaining standing is nothing to the effort of resisting being overwhelmed with anxiety. I don't want to read on. The word 'Legacies' has thrust itself from the page into my mind, triggering a distant memory somewhere in the fog inside there.

'Dear Mrs Fairman,
We write in respect of the property owned jointly by yourself and your son, Mr Max Fairman.'
Now that Mr Fairman has reached the age of twenty-five it is our duty to transfer ownership of half the house to him, in accordance with the instructions issued to us by yourself and your late husband, Mr Conor Fairman.'

The jolt in the pit of my stomach reminds me that Max's birthday was last week. Twenty-five. He turned twenty-five years old five days ago, whilst I was languishing in bed. Max will own half of the house and its land once I sign the attached form.

I am blind as I half-walk, half-stagger to the bench. I grip the letter, oblivious to its flames of heat searing my hands. I see nothing and feel only bile churning in my stomach. Once the transaction is made Max can do what he likes with the house, and he has made clear what it is he wants to do. I wonder if he had known all along whether his fawning last visit had in fact been an opportunity for me to hand it over to him before this happened. He has won again.

I remember the conversation with Conor after we had lived in the house for a few weeks. He so wanted children to fill the house with that he asked me if we could make a trust for them to ensure they could take it over when we could no longer look after it, probably when they were twenty-five, he had argued. I had laughed at him. These children did not even exist then, and we certainly had no other assets to leave them. That was exactly the point, he had argued, we could give them a gift to be born with and instil a love of what will one day be theirs by raising them to love its walls and gardens. We had visited the solicitor's office, who, although looking askance at us, had drawn up the required documents, which with a smile and flourish each of us had signed. When Conor died, these must have been updated to include Max's name. I had no memory of it but neither did I of any of the other dozens of documents that I had signed then.

The new shoots of energy that Rosie's food gave me wither and die and I drop the letter to the floor, following it as it skids away from me towards the entrance to the room I had not entered since Max vacated it. I stamp on it with both feet in a futile dance of rage. I kick at the door to the room, shouting Conor's name at the top of my voice and then beat the door with my fists as the sobbing starts.

The words deaden against the wooden panelling and I squat down, head in hands crying. Then, anger not yet satiated, I jump up and dash the keys, letters, candle and vase from the hall table in a satisfying crash to the floor. I feel destroyed and I want to destroy. I look around for more destruction to reap. The hall is sparse but as images of Conor and Max swirl together in my head I remember the photos on the kitchen dresser. I stride to the stairs and leap them in two strides. In the kitchen I pick up the pictures of a dour-looking Max from the dresser, smash its glass with my fist to rip the face in two, three, five pieces, and toss the pieces to the hard, tiled floor.

The images in my head are replaced with voices that bounce around, taunting me: 'You should never have come here, you don't deserve happiness, you should have known that.' I scream back at them, 'Why must I be the person who lost everyone she loved and then everything she loved? Why does it have to be me?' until my body is exhausted and my mind is in a disarray of numbness and rage. As I slump to the floor against the kitchen wall, I feel dissociated, floating above myself, until prickles and chills on my skin land me back down with a jar. The images of the letter, of Conor, of Max, swirl around my helpless self. The quiet of the house feels threatening – Max could appear at any time to sneer his success at me. I dread to hear the silence being broken by a smug Max and even when leaden steps take me back up to the bedroom I check behind me and listen for his footsteps. I know it cannot be long before he comes in triumph to tell me there is nothing more I can do. Perhaps if I lie here for long enough a blessed peace will come, and Max can have all he wants without me knowing about it. I will not have to see the destruction of the house, the uprooting of its natural environment, houses being built where once there were trees and grass. Perhaps if I am in eternal sleep, Max's greed, relishing every plunge of the digger into the wild, natural paradise of its gardens will mean nothing to me. He will not care if I am no longer around. We will never be reconciled now, and with me out of the way he will own the whole house and all of its surroundings and I will not have to endure my sadness at his actions.

But I am not ready to give in completely yet. I won't make it easy for Max by dying and leaving his life forever. I force myself to think through any remaining options I have. With his ownership of half the house they are limited and I will have no power to stop him doing what he wants on his half, but the idea of living here whilst such desecration is going on around me is horrific. Perhaps I can start up a campaign to prevent the building work taking place, like Rosie did all those years ago before Donal's death. Enjoying the vision for a moment it wasn't long before I knew that Max would only laugh at me and order the machines to go round me, I picture myself standing firm in front of advancing bulldozers, but then the gossips who have always thought of me as a reckless mother will have a field day over the scandal of a mother openly fighting a losing battle with her child. No doubt more of our secrets would be exposed and those people will be able to congratulate themselves on how right they have been all along to have seen me as a dysfunctional influence on Max and his father. I am empty, drained of ideas. Talking to Max will be pointless, denying him access futile.

'What would Rosie do?' I muse out loud.

I hear her calm, reasoned voice encouraging me to think rationally, to accept what I cannot change, to pick my battles. Is this a battle I have to concede?

I lie back down, thinking back over our many conversations, remembering stories of her own children's antics told to me at the market stall. I recall long afternoons sitting in her cosy kitchen talking about everything and nothing, of meeting Bella for the first time and of Rosie's kindness in taking her in. My mind wanders to the afternoon we spent on the lawn here, sitting on a scratchy blanket in bright sunshine, enjoying each other's company, trying to work out who Bella really was by asking about where she lived, and ending up having to invent her life for ourselves. How we played at millionaire interior decorators for this house, developing themes for each room, restructuring bathrooms and landscaping the garden, laughing at our fantasies. Then, clear as anything, I recalled Rosie's words, spoken half in jest with just a touch of envy:

'Am I the only person who lives in an two-up, two-down ordinary house?'

I picture the rows of houses that make up the town. All so similar in structure but distinguished by their different pastel colours, ornamental doorknobs, window decorations. Nestled close to each other with well-tended gardens back and front, they have always made me grateful for my space but given me pangs of envy at not having a community around me. Rosie's words take on a new meaning. Maybe I am just like everyone else. Maybe I too can live in an 'two-up two-down ordinary house' in the town, personalise it, make it my own with no threat from Max. Have tea with the neighbours, help them out when they are in trouble, call on then for support. Maybe that is the answer. Maybe I was never meant to find happiness in this house of false dreams. To admit defeat to Max, hand it over and start life again in a new place as a new woman may be the only chance of ever finding contentment.

This clarity of thought is such a relief that I don't allow myself to think of anything other than how to make it real. I do not think about how I will have to clear away the remnants of my life with Conor and Max, leave my beloved kitchen garden, give up my lake swims. I certainly do not think about the inevitability of Max's pleasure at his victory. I will do whatever I have to do to convince myself that this decision is the correct one. To start with, that means talking to Rosie.

#

When I enter Rosie's kitchen an hour later, washed and with hair brushed, a ghostly figure hurls itself across the room at me and clutches me in a tight embrace. Disentangling myself, and brushing flour from my clothes, warmth flickers inside me, as it always does when I see Rosie.

'Where have you been love? Is everything ok?' says Rosie, oblivious, as usual, to the streaks of white on her face, in her hair and down her crimson red dress.

'Well, no it's not really, Rosie,' I say, as the tears come.

Letting her guide me by the shoulder to a chair where she places the usual cup of tea in front of me with a plate of still-warm brownies, I search for words as she speaks.

'I knew something was wrong. I just knew it. I came to find you, you know. I think you were home actually, but that you needed to be alone. Am I right? Do you want to tell me what's been going on. Come on, fill me in, I haven't seen you for a week and a half.'

Rosie leans across the table, looking at me with caring expectation in her eyes.

'Oh Rosie, there is so much to say. Bella is living in the woods, I am about to lose the house, Max hates me, and I am angry with Conor. And that's just for starters.'

The words tumble over each other as they spill onto her kitchen table. As ever, Rosie knows exactly what to say.

'Whoa, ok. So I was right, there has been loads going on. I knew it was not like you to disappear for so long without a word. What has Max done now?'

So, I tell her about Max's victory, How I had forgotten about the legacy of the house ownership but that Max so clearly had not. I tell her how I see now how deceitful he had been in trying to win me over with wheedling and lies, knowing all along that half of the house would soon be his. I tell her how I have banished him forever from my life.

When I finish, breathless, I wait for a look of horror to cross her face. She has listened to my tale, without saying a word, to my descriptions of failed motherhood, to the account of a life unravelling. She encouraged me only with her eyes to tell her everything. Now though there is not a look of horror but of compassion reflecting back to me. I can hardly bear to receive it and look down at the floor. It is as though the final death throes of the guilt and anger that have had their tendrils wrapped around me for so long are wrestling each other there. As they fight for survival and I bathe in the comfort of Rosie's acceptance, they seep away through the floorboards until there is only empty space at my feet, space to be filled with whatever I choose.

I want to start with accepting that I will lose my house, to tell Rosie that I am going to move into the town, but I hesitate. I need her agreement that this is the right thing to do. The familiar resident butterflies in my stomach have woken up and are fluttering around, knowing that when I say that my decision is made it will be hard to go back, but I cannot face the agony of indecision anymore. I don't have left any will to fight. If Rosie tells me it is not the right thing to do I will sink into useless despair again at the prospect of having to reconsider what now seems so clear to me. I take in a sharp breath through my nose.

'So, I have decided to move out of the house and into town. I want to live away from where Max can influence me anymore, away from the poison that we have created between us, and away from any view of the destruction that he plans to carry out.'

'So, is this about you and Max?' Rosie asks, and then, with insightful wisdom, 'Or is it about Conor?'

Her soft brown eyes gaze at me, non-judgemental, wise, and caring. I want to melt into them. How lucky her daughters are to have Rosie as a mother. I realise then that my relationship with Rosie is the closest to a maternal one that I have ever had. She must have heard all the rumours about me, been told that I am no good and an irresponsible mother. Perhaps she has even been vilified herself for associating with me, but she has stood by me regardless for all these years. How I wish I had been able to do that for my son. Rosie has listened to me, advised me, and yes, cared for me, without ever criticising or berating me. I long to lean over the table and hug her.

The simple question Rosie asked has helped me to understand the confusion of the last few days. I can see now that the threat to the house that Max poses his actually a threat to my last links with Conor. I am scared that I will no longer have the memory of him, of our life together if I lose the house, and without those what do I have? I am petrified that I will be just a lonely, middle-aged, single woman and failed mother. The tears of self-pity start to fall, dripping down my nose, unconstrained and not wiped away.

'You are right, Rosie, it is about Conor. I am so frightened of losing my last connection with him.' I look at her as I say, 'but I have already lost it haven't I?'

'But giving up the house does not mean giving up the memories of all that Conor and you had does it?' Rosie retorts, 'Moving into town only puts different bricks around you, not a different history, doesn't it?'

I want to believe her, to be confident that losing the house does not mean that all I had with Conor will be lost also, but in that moment I don't know if I can.

As we continue to talk though, something shifts inside me. I start to sense a change deep in my mind. With it I hear my voice becoming stronger, more animated, and the words come faster. Gradually, I am no longer hoping but believing that I have the answers to Rosie's questions.

'If I find a house in town I can make it my own., decorate it and make it cosy. With a little garden I can grow my vegetables. I will be able to continue to have my stall at the market. I could even look for a second job. And I'd be living closer to you.'

A picture of the new independent me begins to take shape with my words. I will be free from obligations and worry. I will live in a comfortable, peaceful house done up just for me. The only silences there will be created by me, not by the ghosts of Conor or the shadow of Max. I will find strength to stand up to those who judge me with false knowledge. I will meet people who will know nothing of my past and I can be who I want to be with them. The butterflies in my stomach have begun to soar and glide in my stomach and the tingle lightens my mood.

'Yes! That's more like it girl, positive and energetic,' says Rosie. 'There is so much more to you than being a widow and a mother. Ever since I have known you I have believed that but you needed time, and a few crises, to find out for yourself.'

She jumps up and rounds the table to give that longed-for hug. We hold each other in an embrace of love and freedom, acceptance and joy. It fills my whole body and warms through me. I can do this, start a new life and carry only what I want of the old one with me. I am liberated.

When we eventually separate and take our seats again, we talk more, and Rosie shares a story about her life that I have never heard.

'Don't get me wrong, I know myself from losing Jerry how hard it is to start out alone, to begin life as a different person to the one you thought you were or the one you wanted to be.'

Her eyes glisten as she recalls her early life as a married mother of two children. I can imagine the excitement and enthusiasm with which she embraced it as a young woman. As she talks I see the tall, strong farmer who loved his family and his work. The world they created together had been idyllic until a farming accident destroyed his body and changed their life. She tried to nurse him back to wholeness, but he died of his injuries. She told me that the worst thing for her was witnessing his despair at not being able to care for her and the girls anymore. As she tells the story she has a far away look in her eyes. I know that I may as well not be there as she transports herself back to her own time of hopes and expectations.

When she finishes neither of us say a word as the tragedies in our lives swirl around the room. We sit for a while, until Rosie brushes at her face and says, 'Right, ok, so you are going to move to a new house.'

I raise my head and return Rosie's look.

'Come on, let's go into the living room and get on the computer. It's time to go house-hunting,' she says, snatching up a bottle of wine and two glasses.

Chapter 11

We are down to the last dregs of the bottle, and have found three potential houses for me, each one small and well-presented in the middle of town. My favourite has a small shed in the garden with a view of grazing pastures. It is easy to imagine myself setting up my studio there, being inspired by the scenery to make vividly coloured quilts, and jewellery that reflects the multigreen landscape.

Tiring of sitting leaning over the computer on two upright chairs at the desk, and agreeing that there is little more we can do tonight, Rosie and I move to the sofa. Unlike the one in the kitchen, this one, less used and banned from dogs, has retained its springiness. It encourages me to sink back against its array of cushions, wine glass in hand, and relish the lifting of the weight of disappointment and futility that has buried me for so long.

'So, what were you saying about Bella living in the woods?' Rosie says with an abruptness that startles me out of my reverie.

'You can ask me yourself.'

We both sit upright from our slumped positions, taken by surprise to see Bella at the living-room door.

'Bella, hi, come in,' says Rosie.

I try to supress the flush of embarrassment, thinking that Bella might have caught us gossiping about her.

'Come here, Bella, squeeze in,' I say, patting the plump sofa space between us. 'Rosie and I have been catching up.'

Bella looks a little hesitant, but moves to sit with us, moving across the room in her light-footed way so that she is beside us before we have each shuffled sufficient distance apart to make space for her. She sits on the edge of the cushion bouncing slightly as our weight redistributes across the sofa.

'Can't tempt you with a glass of wine I don't suppose?' says Rosie.

Bella smiles as she shakes her head and turns to look at me.

Her look is intense, sees right into me. I shiver a little, feeling that she knows exactly what I have been going through these last few days. In my recent well of self-pity I had not given her much thought but now in the cosiness of Rosie's living room I can imagine that she has been watching over me from her home in the woods, seeing everything that I have been going through and waiting for a chance to console me. The feeling is not frightening, more one of being protected. After our night in the woods Bella knows more about me and my life with Conor, than anyone else other than Rosie. In witnessing my longing for Conor, she saw me at my most vulnerable, but it did not feel threatening, and I was pleased to have her with us.

'I am sorry you have been so distressed,' she says, almost whispering the words.

'What?' I say a little too loudly, 'Thanks, I'm ok. I'm alright now,'

Bella sighs and looks away, reorganising her tiny body on the sofa whilst Rosie leans around her to top up my glass. I gulp a mouthful and lean my head on the cushions behind me.

'Well anyway, I was just about to tell Rosie about you living in the woods, Bella, but maybe you can explain it better than I can?'

'Oh do, Bella, do' says Rosie, 'it sounds rather perfect. No cooking and cleaning, nobody wanting anything from you. Free to do as you wish. I can see why you live there.'

Rosie's smile releases Bella and, starting hesitantly, words begin to tumble from her cherubic lips.

'I like living in the woods. I feel close to nature and at peace. It is the only place in this world that I feel happy. It feels like home.'

She looks sad as she speaks, and Rosie and I glance at each other, as Bella continues.

'I believe that nature will provide for us all if we treat her with respect. She brings much to celebrate and helps keep life in balance.'

These sombre words are not in keeping with the easy banter between Rosie and I that had preceded her arrival. They remind me of the impending destruction to nature that Max is about to wreak, and I wriggle in my seat, taking another gulp from my wine glass, as the uncomfortable thoughts intrude back into my head.

'When nature is offended though her wrath is great,' Bella goes on. 'She can destroy lives and crops, animals become sick and humans suffer, so when I live with her I do what I can to support and protect all that she does. I see nature as the child I couldn't raise.'

As she says these, Bella's looks directly at me and pierces me with her cornflower blue eyes.

'I know that you understand, Marianne.'

She's wrong though, I can't understand what Bella is saying. I clear my throat in embarrassment.

'Well, gosh Bella, it is certainly clear why you love living in the woods,' I know my words are clumsy, and Rosie looks at me, brow furrowed, before turning to Bella.

'What about the person you are looking for Bella? How are you getting on with your search?'

I had forgotten about Bella's quest. She never mentions it and still neither Rosie nor I have any idea of who she is looking for.

'I have not found him,' she says. 'But in the woods I feel I am closer to him.'

I wedge myself back into my space at the end of the sofa as the potential of this conversation draws me back in.

'Perhaps we can help,' says Rosie. 'Who is it you are looking for? I know most people in the town. If he is here we can probably locate him.'

Bella takes a moment, and then looking across the room and not at either of us whispers, 'My son.'

Rosie and I lock our gaze in wide-eyed surprise until I manage to say

'Who is he, love? What's his name?'

'I don't know.'

The look of anguish on her delicate face is enough to bring me to tears.

'I don't know his name, where he is, what he is doing. He doesn't even know that I am his mother.'

Something terrible must her happened for her to have lost this nameless child. I want to help her, to join her in her search for him. I want to know why she has lost him, why she has never told us about him before. What happened?

As I struggle to find words, Rosie wraps her arms around Bella, and strokes her back, 'Oh love.'

I pat awkwardly at a part of Bella's shoulder that is not smothered in Rosie's embrace. When Bella starts talking again her voice is muffled but as her tale unfolds her voice strengthens as she tells us her story.

'When I was sixteen, I ran away from school to spend the weekend at a music festival. It was amazing. I loved the freedom of being surrounded by happy carefree people, and of course the music blending with the gorgeous scenery. On the last night I was sitting on the riverbank, just watching and listening, feeling happy and content but worried about having to return and face an entirely different kind of music. I was determined to make the most of what I was sure would be my last night of freedom for a very long time. A man came up to me and asked if he could sit with me. He seemed a bit confused, asking me where he was and who the other people were. At first I assumed he was drunk or on drugs, but as we started to talk I realised he was genuinely confused and lost. He told me he had heard the music from across the fields and had felt compelled to follow it. His confusion wasn't an unhappy one he said, he felt enchanted and spellbound by the music, the dancing, all the happy people. To me, it seemed like we were kindred spirits, both lost in the world outside this one, and happy to surrender to the serenity offered to us by the festival that night.

We had a magical evening, sometimes sitting in silence, sometimes walking through the crowd to find new music, staying together, comfortable in each other's company. It was as though a spell had been cast over us so that nothing mattered, not our lives away from here, who we were or what was going to happen the next day. When the music finished, and night began to settle, it seemed only natural to wander back to my tent and spend the rest of the night together.'

Bella was staring into the distance as she relived her happiness, until with a sniff she continued her tale.

'I didn't question what I was doing. I felt safe and cared for by him. I had been feeling alone for a long time and we had a wonderful night, one I will never forget. We fell asleep as dawn was breaking but when I woke up, hot and clammy from the midday sun burning through the tent walls, he was gone. I was alone. There was nothing to show he had ever been there and although I looked for him amongst the dwindling crowd of festival goers packing up and leaving the field, I couldn't find him. Eventually, I left too, not quite believing whether what I remembered was true or not'

Bella turned to look at Rosie and me. She was shaking, and the pink glow of her flawless sallow skin belied the upset she was feeling at telling her story. Her distress was contagious, and I was torn between telling her not to tell us anymore and my sense that she wanted to finish her story. I confess to some curiosity too, and I said nothing.

'I realised I was pregnant a few weeks later. It hadn't been a dream. The reality of my changing body told me, and and the teachers at school, what had happened. I dreamt a new dream then, one of becoming a mother, having my own baby to rear and love. Someone to give my life meaning and a future. But it was not to be. There was no choice as far as my parents were concerned – they told me I wouldn't be capable of raising a child, that they wouldn't help me, and it was only the right thing to do to put the child up for adoption as soon as he was born.'

The air in Rosie's sitting room was taut with sadness and tension as the three of us sat motionless.

'On the day that he was born… 'Bella's words stuck in her throat 'He was so tiny. Brown and wrinkled, with a shock of red hair. The most beautiful baby I had ever seen. They took him from me straightaway and my heart broke. I thought I would never have the chance to tell him I loved him, to feel his soft new skin on mine. I thought his new parents were waiting in the hospital to take him away there and then but when I calmed down the kind nurses explained that I would have a few hours with him before he was given to his new parents. They promised they would bring him back to me as soon as he was weighed and washed, and sure enough after what felt like a lifetime, they placed a clean, sleepy baby back into my arms, along with a bottle of formula to feed him with.'

Her words petered out as the heavy silence draped itself around us. I remember my adoration of Max on our first day together. My desire to tend to his every need, to smother him with love and hold him so close to me that nothing and no one would ever threaten the love between us. I remember falling asleep with his hand in mine, overwhelmed with responsibility and the urge to care for him. The idea of being told to give him away would have been unbearable.

'I knew these hours were precious and I held him so close as I tried to feed him,' Bella continued, 'but something was wrong. He started wriggling and squirming, he wouldn't take the bottle. It was like he was trying to get away from me. I struggled to keep him close and cried with him as his wails got louder. I was hot, sweating, desperate to have final precious time with him. The nurses tried to help but only made things worse – he was like a wild, wild creature. He didn't feel part of me anymore. I became distraught. Shouting at him, at the nurses, berating myself, until suddenly in the middle of this chaos, it struck me – this was not my baby. This frantic screaming bundle hated me. He knew I was not his mother, that a mistake had been made. My own baby was somewhere else, swapped with this one. He knew it and I knew it, but no one would believe me. They tried to assure me that he had been attended to for all the time he was away, that there was no way the identity bracelets could have been confused with another child. But I knew, I knew, this was not my child. In despair and hopelessness, I pushed him from me and the nurses stepped in and took him. I never saw him again.'

Rosie and I are silent, each contemplating the horror of this story. Bella sobs quietly, tears running down her face. To lose a child this way, to believe she had no chance to say goodbye, was a double bereavement, almost too shocking to comprehend. Bella's glistening eyes implore, sympathy and understanding from us., not trusting that she has already been given it. Neither Rosie nor I could blame her.

I so want to give Bella what she wants, to show her care and acceptance. To believe her story, acknowledge her pain, share it, take it away. I let her down though. One part of me feels so desperately sorry for her but another part abandons her, and dwells only on me. Perhaps Max was not my child? Perhaps I had been given the wrong child back in the hospital? Did we both know we didn't belong to each other all along? I am wrenched from sympathy to confusion. Of course I feel for Bella: to twice lose a child against her will, live a life filled with such loss is unimaginable, but Max has been lost to me too from the day I took him home. What if he had been given to me in error? What if he wasn't my child? Could that be the explanation for his rejection of me, or mine of him? Does this explain my life of guilt and regret?

Bella is speaking again, and I try to shake these fantastical thoughts.

'When a friend's baby died a little while ago, and I saw her suffering, a yearning for my own child was released from that secret locked place in my heart. I longed to see him again and decided to come and look for him. All I know is that the hospital is close to here, but I don't know where to begin to search for him. Or even that I will know him if I see him.'

'Then we must help you,'

There is no hesitation from Rosie as she desperately tries to assuage the awful feelings of hopelessness that Bella's story has provoked.

The three of us spend the next hours discussing who Bella's son might be, what he might look like, where the father may be. I force myself to accept her story, to forget my own, to push from my mind the grabbing thoughts of explanation for my own motherhood experience. Bella has few details to help in the search but feeling like we can be of help to Bella is satisfying and drags my mind from the many questions. Accidental baby swaps happen, and the mothers always know when a child is not their own. Even the short time Bella had with her own son could have been enough for her to recognise that the replacement baby was not hers. Had I failed to recognise that in Max? Yes, we would do all that we could to help Bella find her son and mend the broken heart she has been carrying since his birth. And yes, I will not let myself dwell on what simply cannot be, in trying to understand what has gone so wrong in my relationship with Max. Yet in the hour of the wolf, when I startle myself awake at 3.00am and lie with alone with my thoughts and the darkness, the questions come racing back. Max was born in the same hospital as Bella's baby, was my child swapped with hers? Did I let him out of my sight? Did he seem like a different baby even before

I left the hospital? I can't remember. I can never remember, and straining to relive that time leaves me exhausted each time, until I fall into deep sleep, and the dreams sneak in; dark forests, receding figures, creatures washed up by the sea grabbing at me. I always see myself in the dreams, reaching out, calling, chasing, but can never quite make out who it is I am so desperate to connect with.

Chapter 12

Yesterday I looked again at the solicitor's papers finalising the handover of half of the house to Max. I laid them out on the kitchen table, reading once more the legalese and placing an x at each dotted line requiring signatures from Max and me. I had just got to the end when I heard the front door being slammed open with such force that it rebounded on its hinges. Each pounding footstep was matched with a pound from the beat of my heart until he was in the doorway of the kitchen with a smirk on his face.

'Mother, have you signed the papers yet? You know you have no choice don't you? I gave you every opportunity to do it the easy way but no, your stubbornness has caught you out. You must hand over half the house to me now and I can do what I want with it. It's over, Mother, and I win.'

The smirk spreads across his face, drawing the skin taut and showing the ugliness of his empty eyes.

'I'm doing it right now, Max,' I say quietly.

His mouth sets into a rictus grin as he rounds the table to lean over me at the papers laid out on the table. I pick up the pen I had placed by their side.

'Marianne, I'm sorry to intrude but the front door was open… Oh,' Bella is at the door of the kitchen, bewildered by the scene of this man looming over my bent form.

Max whirls round to face her. 'Who are you?' he barks.

'Marianne?' Bella cocks her head around Max's body to look at me.

'This is Max, Bella, my son. He has come to demand that I sign half of the house away to him so that he can build on the land and turn this into flats.'

I look at Bella, hoping for a response that matches my aggressive tone. Bella of all people will know how much I resent the planned destruction, but she seems not to have heard me. As she had edged closer to me, trying to get around Max's menacing form, the two had caught each other's eyes. They both looked quizzical, Max's face had twisted out of its ugliness and into a curious stare, Bella's eyes were squinting, giving her a frowning look.

'Bella?' I say.

She turns her head with such speed that it looks as though she has been hit.

'Yes? Sorry, yes, Marianne,' she stutters.

'Max is my son,' I repeat. 'He is here to ensure that I sign the papers handing half of the house over to him so that he can build on the land and divide the house into flats.'

Turning to Max she asks, 'Why do you want to do that? This is the most gorgeous old house around. It's been here for over two hundred years. It was never meant to be divided up. It was built for a chieftain. It would be the perfect family home for someone.'

'Yes, for the perfect family,' Max spits back, with a glare at me.

'Max!' I intervene, shocked at his rudeness to this woman he has never met before. It makes no difference.

'Mum and I had a go at that didn't we, Mum?' He turns to me with a fake smile, 'I said didn't we, Mother?' His voice is cold and harsh, accusatory. 'But that didn't work out so well did it? A dead father who I never knew and a mother who wishes I was not her son.'

'That's not true, Max,' I say, my voice quavering with uncertainty.

I turn to the papers again, preparing to make the marks that will change my life. My heart thumps at my chest and the pen slips in my sweaty hand. This is it. In front of Bella I am signing away the vestige of my dreams.

I cast a questioning look at her and perceive the slightest nod of her head.

It's all I need.

#

As Max swaggers away waving the signed papers above his head, I can't help noticing Bella staring after him as he left, nor that he cast her a brief backwards glance.

'Come on, let's get packing,' she says, 'No need to prolong it now, sweetie. The deed is done, let's get organised.'

As we start sorting through the bedroom, the pile for disposal becoming much larger than the one for 'keeping', she asks me how I am feeling. I start to try and tell her about the strange swirling of relief, sadness, and disbelief that is going on within me but am silenced when she says, 'I wonder what it is like to be Max right now.'.

'Quite frankly, Bella, I don't really care. He has got what he wants so good luck to him.'

'You don't really mean that.'

I sat back on my heels, pausing from going through the drawers containing Conor's moth-eaten jumpers.

'I do. Right now, I do. He has upset me so much in these past few months that I feel nothing for him right now. It's a relief to be free to move on, and a tragedy. I can't bear to think of what he is going to do to this house.'

With a piercing look she says, 'How did it come to this?'

It is a question with a thousand answers, none of them sufficient to capture the rejections, the disappointments, the sadness of my relationship with Max. As I try to explain to Bella the complexities of the lives of two people that were sometimes part of a triad and more often part of a pair, who were supposed to love each other but couldn't, who wanted to accept the other but felt compelled to reject them, I can see she is only half-listening.

'It's like he was born to live a life of loss, right from the beginning,' I say. 'He had to live without a father and then with a father who wasn't available to him and then left him completely. His only support was a mother who was not coping with the loss of her husband and who clung to false hopes and ideals for much of his childhood, always disappointed that they were not met. I put more into his house than I did into him,' I continue.

'He had to cope with further rejection from other children, their parents, other people in the town. It is no wonder that he retreated into his world of bricks and books. Perhaps only there he could find allies and control. For me, raising him has been...'

'Wait a minute,' interrupted Bella, 'tell me more about Max.'

There was a glint of excitement in her eye that did not fit with my mood of contemplation and sense-searching.

'About Max?'

'Yes, what sort of child was he? Was it always difficult with him? Was there never a time when you felt close to him?'

Assuming that Bella was trying to be helpful by pushing me to reflect on the good times as well as the trying ones, I reached back in my mind. I heard myself telling her about my pregnancy, how I had been so determined to give my baby, Conor's baby, the very best from the start so that when Conor returned he would fall in love with our wonderful child immediately. I told her how life outside the house passed me by in my single focus on this growing person inside me. How I believed, like Max, that the world was hostile, and the people in it judgemental, condemning me and my situation. That I had done little to explore it, test it, challenge the views I believed people held about us.

Bella looks enthralled, greedy for more from me, asking me questions about my life with Max. No, not about my life with Max, about Max himself. She wants to know everything about him, what food he liked, how he performed at school, what provoked his behaviour. It was hard for me to talk in such depth about this son I have just lost. The room blurs through my glistening eyes. Talking about him reminds me that the time when I truly loved Max, when I felt that he truly loved me, believed we would be happy together forever, had been so short. In those early days when I was able to cuddle him, try to soothe him, whisper to him as he settled to sleep I did not feel the force of rejection that grew out of our years together. Maybe it wasn't that he was pushing me away by refusing to feed, squirming at my touch, rather that he was using me to seek his understanding of himself, testing me to find his boundaries. How did that set into the hard, unfeeling concrete of resentment toward him? When did I become so worn down that I forgot to consider alternatives to reading his responses to me as rejections? At what point did we settle into the tense, aggressive understanding that he was not for me and I was not for him? Why have I spent so many years thinking Max and I had somehow been thrust together as a cruel joke?

Bella and I were standing together looking out over the grounds of the house now. She still seems distracted and I welcome the interlude in her questioning of me. Yellow flowers from woody plants, leaves too big for delicate stems, crawl across the window, the overgrown wilderness already signalling abandonment and not the benign neglect I thought I had brought to the house. My eyes sweep across the meadow, over the woods to the lake, as I absorb the vista. The feelings of comfort and support I had so often felt from wandering these grounds now grip at my stomach with a malice of confusion. Were they really comforting or were they governing me? Filling me with false security disguised as escape from the nightmare of what was happening inside the house? Those feelings of freedom and liberation that 'the Context' brought... I snap myself back to the room. Even calling it the Context sounds nonsensical now. Those grounds were simply nature and had offered me escape for all these years, but why did I need to be supported and protected by them? They were just nature doing what nature does, but my life with Conor and Max had been tragedy after tragedy culminating in failure. What had it all been for? Why did I ever think that a vegetable garden would be enough to grow love when I could not grow it myself?

I stumble slightly as the two of us turn from the window. I fall against Bella as she guides me to the foot of the bed, where we sit on the floor, heads leaning against the mattress behind us.

'Tell me more about Max.'

'Really Bella, I am trying to move forward. I want to forget the pain of my life in this house. I am not sure that it helps talking about Max.'

I am trying to stay patient with her insistence.

'It might help, Marianne, keep talking.'

The glint of curiosity and excitement has returned to her eyes and feels intrusive. I don't need her here to help me pack, and I don't want her here if she is going to push me into talking about things I don't want to talk about. I have believed for years, most of Max's lifetime, that he is the source of all of my pain. If I hadn't been pregnant with him maybe I would have noticed something about Conor that warned me he was going to leave. Maybe if I hadn't had a new baby to look after alone, I would have done more to look for Conor? Perhaps if that baby hadn't been so difficult…

'What did he look like when he was a teenager?'

Something inside me gives way to irritation. I cannot understand why she is so interested. Why she is questioning me so relentlessly about Max. She has met him for the first time on one of the worst days of my life and seems to have little time for me, only interest in him. How strange her behaviour is. I turn my head to look at her, seated beside me on the floor. She returns my scrutiny with a look so intense that the cog turning in my mind is almost physical. The seed that planted itself when Bella had told Rosie and me about having to give up her son, started to scratch at the mud of emotions in which it was buried.

'Bella, what is going on? Why are you so interested in Max?'

Bella lowers her eyes as the cogs clunk into place.

'You don't think…' The words choke in my throat.

Her eyes raise to meet mine and I know that the seed has sprouted.

'You think Max is your son?'

It is a surreal moment. Here am I on the verge of losing everything and about to start a brand-new life with nothing, asking this woman who I have only known for a short time whether she thinks my son is the one she gave up years ago.

Bella's eyes are brimming with tears as she stares through them at me with a longing that stabs at my heart.

'Oh Bella, Bella, surely not? He's not, he can't be…'

'Why not, why can't he be?' she sobs. 'The two of you never got on, you always felt there was something wrong between you. You told me he changed after that first night at home. Maybe a swap took place that night?'

'Stop, Bella, stop. This is madness.'

I have to end this. It makes no sense. Of course Max is not her child. How could my baby not be my baby, have been taken from me and substituted with a monster? This is crazy.

And yet, yet it could explain so much. Those feelings that Max and I were not meant to be together, that our relationship was not one forged by nature but by duty and demand. It could explain that change in Max's temperament, his anger. I have to push these thoughts from my mind. I get up and start to pace the room, throwing glances at Bella who is sobbing into her hands as she cradles herself on the floor at the end of the bed.

Crazy talk, nonsense, as mad as all the stuff about fairies and changelings. It cannot be. No, I have to accept that I was just a hopeless mother and Max suffered because of it. There cannot be any other explanation. I must accept this and resist the temptation of believing it was not all my fault.

'Bella, I am very sorry for you, but this has to stop.'

I am abrupt, unfeeling. I want Bella to go, to take this grenade she has thrown and leave me to grieve over my life as I prepare to start a new one.

'It may be best if you leave, Bella. I can finish the packing on my own.'

Her sobbing does not alter in tone or rhythm as she pushes herself up from the floor with one hand, the other uselessly swiping at her eyes, which avoid mine.

When she is upright, both hands drop to her sides, her head hangs, her face streaked with grey where the tears have marked her porcelain features. We look at each other without saying a word. It is as though our minds are talking to each other.

'It could be you know.'

'It would explain so much.'

'Who says it isn't?'

The seed is a fully grown plant in my mind, its tentacle leaves stretching upwards for the light, poking my thoughts, weaving themselves around my senses.

'It can't be, it can't be, it….'

The door is flung open with such intrusion into this other dimension that both Bella and I jump. Max is there, filling its frame, with one arm outstretched holding those damn papers, looking like an angry version of Conor.

'Found you. You left out one signature, Mother, very clever, nice try, but I spotted it. Can you sign it now, please.'

His voice is full of menace as he waves the papers under my nose.

'Right here if you don't mind, I've brought a pen so no reason to delay.'

Forcing myself to look at the papers and then at Max I snap. 'Where? Where do I need to sign?'

Hand shaking, I reach for the pen he is holding out to me and snatch the papers with my other hand. I walk over to the window to lean on its sill. I can hardly scribble quick enough. I want no more of this house.

'Max, I think you are my son.'

Bella's small voice ripples across the room as time seems to stop. Max halts his stride and turns to face her, as though he has only just noticed she is there.

'What?' comes the retort after a silence that lasted a lifetime.

Bella stares at him, starts to walk towards him. Max backs away.

'Get away from me, mad woman. What are you doing?'

She continues her advance, now with one petite arm outstretched upwards towards his face.

'Max, I think you may be the son I had to give away.'

'What a load of rubbish. How on earth do you expect me to believe that?' Max accuses both of us, his eyes blazing with a viciousness of confusion as they sweep from Bella to me, over and over as he tries to make sense of what is being said.

'I know, we know, it sounds mad, it's hard to believe but…'

'Now hold on Bella,' I interject. 'That's enough.'

'Have you both lost your minds?' says Max. 'Where on earth have you come up with this crazy idea from? Are you drunk? I mean come on.'

His reddened face puckers at the forehead and his lips are tight, strained, pushing his nose into a sharp point as his anger rises.

'Max, you are my son. You are the child that resulted from the union between me and your father, Conor,' Bella stutters.

She turns to me, 'I'm so sorry, Marianne. You may never forgive me.'

My heart thumps and my stomach churns. This woman is convinced that she slept with my husband, became pregnant by him, and exchanged my baby for hers.

'I met him at a festival and spent only one night with him. When I found out I was pregnant I panicked. I was alone in a community that did not allow for union with outsiders. I knew I could not keep you and I knew that I would be found out.'

'Pah,' spat Max, 'You could have slept with anybody, how do you know it was my father, huh?'

Max's upper lip curled as he stared at Bella, head tilted. Then, as the churning in my stomach threatens to reach my throat, I realise that I had not asked her this same question.

She is looking at me and not at Max as she fumbles in the deep pocket of her flowing dress.

'I'm sorry, Marianne, I took this when we were packing up.' Bella produced the photo of Conor that I had stuffed into my bedside drawer after he had died.

'It's definitely him. I knew it the moment I saw this picture.'

She holds it up and I see Conor smiling out of it. The churning inside me settles into ripples of gentle waves as Max too stares at the picture of his father. His lips quiver and his whole body seems to sag. His sadness is etched into every quivering part of his face but before I can reach to comfort him his anger rouses itself again

'You are spiteful, wicked women. What are you trying to achieve here? This is all nonsense and I refuse to believe it. Even I would not stoop to these depths to get what I want. This is all about the house isn't it?'

'No,' Bella says, 'it's not about the house, Max, but Marianne has told me about your plans, your plans for its destruction. We cannot stop you but choosing to hurt her this way will be a decision that you will have to live with for the rest of your life.'

The silence in the room is so thick that I can feel it settling on my hands, my head, in my heart. Here at last is

Max's nemesis. The arbiter of vengeance has confronted him in the tiny figure of Bella, compelling him to live forever with the consequences of his greed. Or to choose to back down and feel forever that he has given in, something Max would never been able to live with.

Hs face reddens as he realises what she is inflicting on him. He can find no words and stutters some meaningless sounds. I am like stone, fixed to the floor and unable to act. For once, though I take no pleasure in watching him squirm, feeling only pangs of something like sympathy for him. My eyes spill tears.

They trickle at first but soon become never-ending streams cascading down my cheeks as I look at Bella, the mother without a child. For all that I feel like I have failed at motherhood, for all the pain and heartbreak that it has brought me, I cannot bear to imagine Max not being my son. I have longed to hold him for so long but he and I broke down all the bridges too long ago to rebuild them in an instant now. I am powerless, and useless to him.

It comes to me with a clarity I have never had before. The pain he inflicts on me will never end until I choose for it to. He feels so hurt by me, so distant and yet so bound to me that he will seek to punish me for the rest of both of our lives. He is slumped against the mantelpiece, no longer leaning on it but being supported by it. I know that if he moves he will fall and every stubborn bone in his body is working to prevent that. This boy, wanted by two mothers, is inured to their love. He had been right all along, he did not belong. He had known it and I had not.

'What a load of tommyrot. I don't know who you are or what has brought you here but if you are asking me to accept that you are my mother, that I should have been brought up by you in some strange nature-loving community, you have got another thing coming. If you think that this a way to get your hands on this house then you are going to have to come up with something better than that.'

187

'You,' he jabs a finger at me, 'you are the person who called herself my mother and look at the pain that has brought me. If you think that I am now going to take on another so-called mother in my life you are very wrong. I gave up on having a mother a long time ago. I gave up on you a very long time ago and I am not about to take on another woman. I don't need a mother, I don't need a wife, I don't need anyone. So if this is something the two of you have cooked up between you, you are going to have to come up with something better than this.'

He pauses to wipe the spittle that leaks from the corners of his mouth as I watch this raving, ranting, forlorn creature through tear-sodden eyes.

'I have employed the developers who will be starting work in a month. You can go, or you can stay and watch your garden being destroyed. It makes no difference to me. This land will become home to all who will pay me for the privilege of living on it. And you know what, Mother? I might just take the best house for myself so that you can watch me building the life I want in front of your eyes. You have a month to decide what you want to do. You can stay or you can go.'

The air shook and rattled through the house with Max's hatred. As he wrenched open the door the bay windows blew open, and with a final bitter look at two battered women, he left.

#

The flowers are still bobbing outside the open window, the wind still blows a gentle breeze and although it is midday, it is as though the darkness that Bella and I are experiencing is living in the room. It mutes the colours of the walls from their faded green into dull grey and blocks the extra slivers of light that try to edge their way through the weave of the tattered curtains. Sadness is palpable, swirling around us, catching on the edges of the open drawers spilling yet-to-be-packed clothes, snarling around the tossed heap of bedclothes pouring from the bed.

Yet, the stillness is a working one. Two worlds have collided between three people and Bella and I sit at the calm centre of the retreating brawl. Around us the possibilities of what might have been loop the loop with the hardness of what was. Love rejected and destroyed clashes with love unrequited and unreciprocated. Secrets and shame rise up to boost the battle and to torture the brevity of hope into oblivion. Bella and I are numbed into passivity, sitting together separately, in spaces that concertina with each new thought.

No part of my body is still, although anyone looking at me would argue otherwise. My blood surges, and my bones shiver, my heart thumps at my chest whilst saliva rises and falls in waves in my mouth. As usual though it is inside my head where the most action is. Far from giving me a way out of my relationship with Max, Bella's story has awakened a new insight that flares with forgiveness and hope. The moment his eyes clouded at the sight of his father in the photograph screamed to me of his lifelong search for belonging. I see with utmost clarity that I do love Max, that I have always loved him. The hurt I felt with every shove from him is nothing compared to his experience of being cast away by his parents. Max's chances at belonging were sabotaged from the beginning of his life born into the mystery of Conor's disappearance. I had been frozen in that void and the consequences brought down destruction and desolation on both of us. All those times I recoiled from his behaviour, thinking myself too wounded to manage it for him, reinforced what he always knew. He was not wanted, not good enough for me. My thoughts whirl in the engulfing stillness, trying to span invisible divides.

I had not been a good mother, had given in to him too often and given up on him too easily and yes, it was my fault. I will never know the motherhood I dreamed of since losing my own mother, but he never had the childhood he deserved. We are both broken but I can now glimpse through the fragments the possibility of having the power to repair.

I look at Bella. The pall of defeat about her face radiates loss, and grief, and guilt. Her eyes are glassy as they look at me with the yearning of a new-born calf. With the events of today she has lost her son again, and like me, has to face herself as a mother without a child. Bella, so in love with nature, has never been allowed to love her own child. We are similar, Bella and I.

We have nothing to say to each other, and when Bella walks towards the doorway I do nothing to stop her.

Epilogue

The air in town feels different to the air around my old house. It smells of the river rather than the sea, and cloaks me rather than lures me. I find it comforting, neutral in its myriad scents of home-cooking, petrol fumes, and swirling freshness rolling in from the surrounding fields. Inside my new house I feel alone and safe. Here, the few photos I brought with me are accompanied by art I have created myself: wall hangings, quilts, battered silver beakers. They enliven the small square rooms and welcome me home when I close the front door on the quiet street outside. The single window of the main room gives me a view of people going about their business in town, but even when they stop outside for a chat with each other, the sound inside is muffled by the low ceiling enclosing my comforting space. I decorate myself too, with jewellery I created just for me, and by wearing the long flowing style of dress that I had so admired on Bella.

Of course, I do not have her petite frame. Mine is slender but taut with firm muscles in my calves and biceps developed from swimming in the sea all year round. Pulling the door to behind me each morning I make the half hour walk to the beach through the empty streets in excited anticipation of the water's caress. The swell of the waves as they push and pull at me, sometimes in play and sometimes in anger, help to cleanse my mind, and when I walk back, hair damp and face shining, I smile at the shopkeepers opening up for the day.

Packing up the old house had been swift and ruthless. Reminding myself of the diminutive size of my new abode made it easier to jettison anything I could. The few bits of furniture that I had acquired, second-hand when bought and now tatty and falling apart, were anyway too large for my new surroundings. I shuddered at the idea of keeping the bed that Conor had languished in for so long and was pleased when it was taken away to be used by people oblivious to its dark past. I did keep those two mismatching armchairs from the bay window and their saggy seats now take up most of the space in my living room behind the front door. I will reupholster them to match the yellow hues I am halfway through painting over the magnolia white with.

Of course my quilts and jewellery came with me, and I also brought the photographs of Conor. The ones from the kitchen dresser and the one that I had hidden away in my bedroom drawer after he died now sit discreetly on a high shelf above the doorway to the kitchen. When I catch sight of them, memories still flood my mind. Our days of abandoning work to head out to the countryside to walk the hills, find hidden beaches, swim, engulf me. I remember again how we found this house, coming across it after running, laughing, across a field of solemn cows, and scrambling over a stone wall, knocking three stones from the resting place they had had for hundreds of years. I can smell again the moss and lichen that smeared our clothes as we fell into the undergrowth of nettles and gorse. I see again our first view of the house, calling us up the meadow of waving grasses and in through its sagging front door. We thought it was welcoming us, enticing us in to fill it with joy and happiness when we stood in that hallway, staring up at the vaulted ceiling and following the sweep of the staircase. I always move swiftly through the door before those memories fade and allow in the more recent ones of illness, death, sadness, and loss that the house brought us.

Other than these things I brought very little, thinking with some degree of malice that it could be Max's job to clear the house when he took it over.

Conor's disappearance has never been explained. Rumours began to circulate a few weeks ago of him having been spotted in London during the time he was gone, living on the streets, drinking and accosting passers-by. I don't believe them. Something broke Conor but when he left me that night he was happy and content. He was not a man about to abandon the life he was building for himself. Something or someone lured him away and destroyed him, played with his mind before spitting him back to me in his quest to find happiness again. In the many tragedies I have experienced I have perhaps learnt one thing – there is not always an answer. Perhaps the fairies did take him. Like Peggy O'Brien, I find some solace in believing this as an explanation.

I sew, paint, and make jewellery still, but now it is not with the frenzy of escape that I used to bring to it. Now, I craft and create in a thoughtful, peaceful manner, relishing the process as much as the final object. The shed in the tiny back garden is my studio, furnished with a woodburning stove, kettle, and a bench taking up the space alongside a long trestle table. My collection of jewellery-making tools grows with the sales of my goods and with each acquisition my contentment grows. I have few material possessions, preferring to come to understand myself through reflection and activity. I volunteer at the local craft shop co-op twice a week where my goods are displayed alongside driftwood sculptures, brightly-coloured ceramics, and children's toys. The other artists and I are a close group, taking it in turns to manage the shop, and working together to promote our endeavours. The thrill of a tourist wandering towards my display and, after fingering a quilt or holding a pair of earrings up to her ears, making the decision to purchase, spurs me on every time it happens.

Having sales at the shop gives me a back-up to my market-stall income. Now if I wake up on a Saturday morning to torrents of rain beating at the window I can decide instead to retreat to the warmth of my studio where the morning passes with no thought of lost income. My self-reliance is not in isolation though. Running the stall also means catching up with people I haven't seen all week, chatting to tourists about the beauty of the town and its surrounding areas, and linking up with Aiden, my on-off barista boyfriend.

Our relationship developed from a hesitant start when he asked me one Saturday to meet him after the market closed. The flutters in my stomach terrified me. I had never known or contemplated a relationship with any man other than Conor and although Aiden and I had spent many hours chatting at his stall or mine, I was wary of becoming close to him. I said no to his first few requests to go out together, making up excuses about having jobs to do at home, but when one day I consented and we sat by the river eating leftover cakes from his stall, I found a new contentment. As we alternated mouthfuls and throwing crumbs to the passing ducks, his interest in how I spend my time, my love of swimming, my fledgling new garden, encouraged me to sound out my new self, to put into words the person I was striving to be. His interest in me was seductive, an opportunity to form an identity based on looking forward instead of backwards. I agreed to meet him again the next week, and then the week after that, until we graduated to having dinner together at his home where he lived with his three dogs.

It felt right and yet threatening. I became fearful that if he knew all that happened in my life he would withdraw, he too might disappear, and so at times I withdrew from him before it could happen. His acceptance and apparent understanding of this need in me is what always pulls me back to him.

Rosie laughs at me, telling me I should accept his interest, not overthink it, go with the flow, hard for me to do at the beginning but becoming easier with every passing month.

Rosie was with me for every step of the move into my new home. She helped me to finish the packing, to transport my few bits of furniture in her truck, and to unpack enough to spend my first night there. She gave me a huge, and now massive, decorative nettle plant to place at the kitchen window overlooking the square of blowsy grasses I am now transforming into a vegetable patch. With every new burst of flame-coloured leaf that this plant produces I see a new shoot in my life; finishing painting the living room in emerald green, completing the turquoise-blue tiling in the bathroom, picking the first crop of beetroot. Each represents a move forward and the replacement of a memory of my old life with a fresh one from my new one.

We never heard from Bella again. When she walked out of Bowlby she walked out of our lives. The maelstrom of confusion that she left behind swirled along with me into my new home, but its force rears up less and less often as time passes. I try to dismiss her from my thoughts, too saddened by her attempt to claim my son as her own and angered by her betrayal of me. I have reason to be grateful to her as well, her story of having a child taken from her unlocked something in me and helps me to understand more about my love for Max. I can see now that it was me that broke the bond between us; my vulnerability could not cope with his tests and I closed myself to him, telling us both that no love existed between us. This was not true. My heartbreak was because of the love that I have for him, my efforts to understand and accept him in the early days laid the foundation for the bond that would keep us together for life. I see him still as flawed and unpleasant but also as lost, misunderstood and needing me. I am still trying to understand that I should not blame him for being how he is. I created him, moulded him, and was the person who showed him the world he inhabits. Perhaps if I had accepted him for who he was instead of fighting him, imploring him to change, to love me, he would not have resented me and felt that he was not good enough. He was right when he said that he was not the son I wanted. I had an image of the child that Conor and I would create, and that image did not include coldness, aggression, withdrawal. I struggled to love the real Max and so, inevitably, he came to struggle to love me. It is as though we were always on parallel train tracks, travelling on the same journey but always apart from each other. It hurts to think he does not love me. It hurts more to question how I have failed in showing him my love.

Perhaps he will never accept me, but I will keep on trying to find the chink into which I can insert promises of acceptance, of openness to him. He lives full-time in the city now. I used to see him at the grounds of the old house when I walked past, hard hat on, barking out instructions. I called out to him once or twice but after a defiant glare in my direction he turned away and resumed ordering the men about. I have written to him recently, a letter of apology and an offer of connection. As yet, I have received no response.

#

Today, a final piece of the puzzle has fallen into place. Dressed in overalls and crouched on the floor to grout the bathroom tiles I hear a knock at the front door. When I open it I see a middle-aged woman, glossy dark hair falling over one shoulder from which hangs a Mulberry handbag. The high-heeled shoes she wears are out of keeping with the usual trainers sported by myself and my neighbours. My first thought is that she must be an official from the council, registering my new ownership of the house or some such.

'Are you Marianne Fairman?'

Her voice is authoritative but tentative. I think I detect a slight quaver in it. A smile plays around her mouth, anxious to disappear.

'I think you knew my sister. Bella.'

The jolt of uncertainty ran through me urges me to deny, but a beseeching look on her face reminds me of Bella's pain and I still my hand from sending her away.

'Bella? Yes, I knew her, I haven't seen her for months though.'

Relief settles on her as she makes to step through the doorway,

'May I come in?'

I can only agree. The room feels smaller than it ever has. We step around each other as I pull a cardboard box of books from one of the armchairs and invite her to sit down.

'I want to tell you about Bella. To explain a little. I believe she was living here a while ago? That she tried to claim your son as her own?'

'Oh yes, but that is all in the past now. I haven't seen her since. I've moved on.'

Dread grips me, I don't want to hear what this woman has to say. Bella is no longer in my life, and Max may be. I don't want anything to disrupt the delicate balance between regret and hope in which I now live. Nothing she can say will help me in my inching forward into my new life.

The woman, though, will not be stopped. In a gentle but assertive manner she insists on telling me a tragic tale of how Bella had been adopted by her parents and then sent away to boarding school so that they could concentrate their devotion on her sister, Colleen, the woman sitting before me. Colleen tells me of her guilt of not recognising the injustice of this, of feeling pleased to be the special child, kept at home to be nurtured whilst her sister lived a hundred miles away, cosseted in an expensive boarding school. She describes the increasing number of reports of Bella's truanting and escapes from the school grounds. Of her turning up at the family home one day begging to be allowed to stay, and of their father bundling her into the car to drive her back to school. Colleen told me that the picture of Bella's face streaming with tears as the car drove off down the road still haunts her.

When Bella arrived home again a few months later, on the day that Colleen received her offer to attend law school, she was angry with her. This day was supposed to be the triumph of all the hard work her parents and herself had put into her life and was being taken over by Bella's intrusion. When Bella screamed at the family that she was pregnant her exclusion from it became complete.

Their mother abandoned the celebratory dinner to start the preparations for Bella to be sent to England to stay with her sister until the baby was born. No contact was kept in those eight months and when Bella returned to Ireland alone, it was only to announce to the family that she would never be troubling them again and was going to search for her baby who had been given up for adoption to an Irish family.

As Colleen talks, I feel like I am living Bella's pain all over again. Waves of remorse flood me as I recall her distress, her determination that Max was her child, and how I had been tempted to provide myself with a way out of my own guilt by contemplating accepting her tale of having taken my baby. It horrified me to think that gentle Bella's quest for a child she had never known was partly true, and that I had eliminated her from my life after her threat to it. That person, the person I was then, was so confused by her own feelings of motherhood she had dismissed those of a friend.

Shaking my head as I try to comprehend what Colleen has told me I ask her why she has come now to tell me this.

'All this happened over twenty years ago. I carried on with my law degree, got married and had a family of my own. In all this time Bella was never mentioned in the family again. My parents expunged her from family history as though their experiment in adopting a child had never happened. But they died a few months ago, within weeks of each other, and I became haunted with a desire to find Bella, to discover what became of her. I was able to use my connections to track her down eventually. It was not easy. She has led a nomadic life, never settling in one place for long and at times disappearing from all records.'

'She used to like living outdoors,' I whisper.

'That would explain it,' muses Colleen, 'but recently she turned up in a psychiatric institution. I was told by a Garda colleague that a distraught woman had been admitted after being found hammering on doors in the city calling for someone called Max. She was taken in for assessment and it was decided to confine her for her own safety.'

Oh how the wheels of misfortune turn I think to myself. Conor, and now Bella, locked away from a world they find so hard to live in, one searching for a way out of it, the other for a lost child within it. Both prevented from searching anymore, in the name of their own safety.

'As soon as I heard I went to visit her,' Colleen continues. 'She was pitiful, aching with the pain of loss, and desperate to be salved with what she is searching for, a child. She holds no malice for me now, rather, sees me as an ally who can help her. I do what I can, I pay for her to live in a comfortable place where the care is excellent. She lives in a world of fantasy, collecting dolls and building miniature houses for them. She has her own patch of garden to tend to in the grounds. But she can never be allowed to be around children. She sees her own son everywhere, and calls out for him day and night, "Max, Max, Max, come back to me."'

The sorrow in Colleen's eyes clouds them as her words fade away. My son's name hangs in the air before it whisks around this house that has so little of him in it. My mind churns with memories of Bella, of Max, of Conor, until I am surprised to feel vindication wash over me. Bella has helped me once again to accept Max. In that stillness with Colleen I am infused with renewed determination to seek him out and work again at reclaiming him as my son. My desire now is to help him to accept me for the imperfect mother I am and to encourage him to take as much love from me as he needs to make up for its lack in his childhood.

As Colleen gathers up her smart handbag and stands tall in her high heels to leave, apologising for having brought this sad story into my life, it is all I can do to hold back the tears that flood out the moment the front door closes behind her.

#

So here I am, new life in place, new me under construction. I have focus and determination and a reason to love. Some of it is directed towards Aiden, a lot of it towards Rosie but most of it is being held in reserve for Max. We will be reunited one day, I cannot bear to think otherwise, and in the meantime I continue to look for ways to appeal to him, entice him back to me so that I can make amends. It is what keeps me going.

As for the old house, that house of dreams, built and shattered on fairy land, it stands proud and decaying in a wilderness that is taking over the grounds as though it had never been tamed. When local bird watchers spotted a rare red-legged chough swooping and soaring, disguised amongst the crows it so closely resembled, there was sufficient cause to halt the development. The dispute continues and I silently thank the fairies for leading this bird off course from its clifftop dwelling place to screech its mocking call to Max and me.

THE END

The Mothers

Lightning Source UK Ltd.
Milton Keynes UK
UKHW012109250621
386167UK00002B/107

9 781800 314634